NOW HE
IS LEGEND

GORDON D. SHIRREFFS

W9-BIS-083

LEISURE BOOKS   NEW YORK CITY

A LEISURE BOOK®

December 1996

Published by

Dorchester Publishing Co., Inc.
276 Fifth Avenue
New York, NY 10001

The name ''Leisure Books'' and the stylized ''L'' with design are trademarks of Dorchester Publishing Co., Inc.

Printed in the United States of America.

NOW HE
IS LEGEND

CHAPTER ONE

THE AFTERNOON HEAT seemed almost molten and there was no wind to move the heavy masses of it that hung over El Corralitos, stifling life and sound like a leaden shroud. A swollen bluebottle fly buzzed lazily between the rusted iron bars of the cell window, in and out, in and out, as though waiting impatiently for the occupant of the cell to die, as the others had died several days ago against the bullet-pocked wall of the shabby old mission building that stood opposite the stinking *calabozo*.

Ross Starkey raised his head. "Get out'a here you hungry sonofabitch," he said huskily. "I ain't ready to join the rest of them. *Viva la revolución! Viva* General Zaldivar, the liberator of Chihuahua! *Viva! Viva! Viva!*"

His voice echoed hollowly in the cell and in the filthy corridor outside of it. The echo died away and there was no other sound except that of the overfed fly. He had eaten well the past week as the barefooted, undersized, overhatted *revolucionarios* died in roped bunches against the mission wall, leaving gouts of blood on the harsh caliche and against the pocked wall of the abandoned mission. Before they had died they had been forced to dig their own graves in the mission cemetery, for at least they had been allowed by the *Federalistas* to lie in consecrated ground, although the mission itself had not been used since the Franciscans had been expelled more than fifty years past by the new republic of Mexico. They had left a heritage; a thick wall to stop the bullets.

Ross sat up and reached for his water dish. A cockroach was feebly swimming in the tepid water, trying to scale the sides of the dish. Ross studied him. "Of all the water in El Corralitos, *cucaracha*," he said thoughtfully, "why does it have to be my dish?" He slipped a nicotine-stained finger under the insect and lifted it out, carefully placing it on the dirty floor. He watched it crawl weakly into the darkness beneath the sagging cot. "Maybe you think that was God, hey? Something huge, so huge you can't imagine *what* it is, suddenly reaches out of the blue and saves your lousy life. What kind of a god do *you* have, *cucaracha*? It can't be a man. Men can't be gods. When they line you up against a wall, my friend, the man facing you with the rifle in his hands is God." He laughed and dropped back on his bunk, covering his burning eyes with his forearms.

"There is salt in that which you say, amigo," said a dry voice from the corridor. Something tinkled musically. Something grated rustily.

Ross sat up. The cell door swung open, protesting stridently on rusted, dirt-clogged hinges. A man walked easily into the cell. His chihuahua spurs were singing softly as they struck the hard-packed earthen floor. The jailer closed and locked the door behind the newcomer. His sandals husked on the corridor floor as he returned to his siesta.

The newcomer eyed Ross from beneath the brim of his heavy felt steeple-crowned sombrero. The sunlight streaming through the barred window glinted dully from the silver trim of the hat. His charro jacket had silver buttons and silver cord had been sewed to the sides of his soft leather trousers. From his ornate clothing to the thin, pencil-line mustache on his upper lip, he was a typical Mexican dandy, of say, perhaps, Chihuahua or Hermosillo, but hardly of El Corralitos.

Ross leaned his sweating back against the peeling wall. "I don't suppose they left you any smokin' or chewin' tobacco, caballero," he said in his cowpen Spanish. He grinned crookedly. "By God, they at least left you your own clothes. You must have connections here in El Corralitos."

The Mexican sat down on the opposite bunk and felt in his shirt pocket. He tossed a pack of Mex ready-mades to Ross. "Keep them, amigo," he said pleasantly. He drew a match against the scabrous wall and lighted Ross' cigarette.

Ross drew in a deep breath of the sweetened tobacco and blew it out through his nostrils. "Mother of the devil," he said appreciatively. "I needed that."

"Could you use a drink?"

Ross tilted his shaggy head to one side. "Water?"

"Brandy."

Ross grinned again. "Sure, amigo," he said dryly. "Send for the waiter. I'll have a platter of *albóndigas* and some *sopapillas* too, while you're being so kind."

The Mexican reached inside his jacket and brought out a silver flask. He unsnapped the top and handed it to Ross. "Helps to drive the stink out of your nostrils," he said.

Ross took the bottle. "There *is* a God," he said fervently. As he raised the bottle to his cracked lips he looked squarely into the Mexican's eyes and an eerie feeling coursed through him along with the good *aguardiente*. He had the lightest damned gray eyes Ross had ever seen, even in an American, and they seemed downright disfiguring for a greaser. The brandy hit him hard. His senses reeled and he almost dropped the flask.

"You all right?" asked the Mexican.

Ross nodded. He held up the flask.

"Go ahead. Don't get drunk," the Mexican said.

"Fat chance," said Ross. He took another slug and took a deep drag on the cigarette. "Maybe God was kind to me because I was kind to that cockroach," he added thoughtfully.

"He won't get you out of here, amigo."

"The only thing that will get me out of here is a firing squad," said Ross. He studied the man. The Mexican was downright handsome. He seemed to have a good lick of the Spanish blood, and a little of the Indian. Maybe he got his gray eyes honestly. There were a lot of "unreconstructed" rebels still living in Chihuahua, Coahuila and Sonora. There had been a time after the war when Ross' old man had wanted to leave New Mexico instead of swearing allegiance to the United States. When he had gotten likkered up enough he would beat the subject to death until Ross' mother had to shut him up.

"Zaldivar never had a chance," said the Mexican.

Ross shrugged. "His money was good."

"How much did he pay you?"

"Twenty dollars a day in gold when there was fighting, five when there wasn't. Food and ammunition on the house. It was a good life while it lasted."

"Where's the gold?"

Ross dropped the cigarette butt to the floor and rubbed it out with his rope-soled sandals, exchanged for his good El Paso boots by the jailer, without benefit of *asking* Ross. Ross fingered a second cigarette. The Mexican tossed a packet of lucifers to him. Ross lighted up. He should have been suspicious right at the start.

"I mean the gold he paid you," added the Mexican. "*Not* his war chest."

Ross blew a smoke ring and punched a dirty finger through it. "The alcalde got his fat hands into that," he said dryly. "Three hundred in gold he said, to pay my way to the border. You can see how far I got."

"That pig would put his mother out to be a whore."

"I wasn't too bright in trusting him," admitted Ross. "My horse died just outside of town. The *Federalistas* were heading for Gran Morelos instead of here. I would have made it except for the alcalde. He held me up until some of Zaldivar's rabble came out of the hills for food and found the *Federalistas'* ambush right outside of here. By dusk that night they had executed at least twenty of them. I happen to know that at least a quarter of them had had nothing to do with Zaldivar."

"God will sort the souls," the Mexican said piously.

Ross leaned back against the wall and brushed the buzzing fly out of the way. "If they planted you in here to worm the location of his contraband guns out of me, you're wasting your time."

The Mexican smiled, revealing perfect white teeth. He lighted a cigarette. "I know nothing of Zaldivar's weapons cache and less of his gold. They say Zaldivar died bravely without revealing the cache of the weapons and the gold. It is said that he had no eyes to see his way to hell when they were through with him. A red-hot iron passed close to the eyes does not help the sight."

Ross shivered a little despite the heat.

"You are feverish perhaps?"

Ross nodded. "I haven't had food for three days."

"No money to pay the jailer, amigo?"

"Like I said: They cleaned me out, from horns to hock." Ross sipped a little of the brandy. It was really hitting him now. "So, you can go back to El Coronel Melgosa, or whoever the hell sent you, and tell 'em I don't know where the gold or the guns are, and I wouldn't tell those greasy sonsofbitches even if they do stand me up against that goddamned wall."

"There are other ways of making you talk," said the Mexican.

Ross bent forward and lifted the back slack of his dirty, sweat-soaked Mex shirt. "Like this, hombre?"

The Mexican whistled softly as he saw the welted purple lash marks. "And you did not talk even then?"

Ross airily waved a hand. He felt ten feet tall with the booze and tobacco smoke in him. "Fact is: they can't beat the truth out of me if it ain't in there in the first place."

The Mexican casually inspected his cigarette. "You're lying, mister," he said quietly in excellent English.

Ross narrowed his eyes. "Say, who the hell are you?"

The man laughed. He reached for the flask and sipped a little of the brandy. He eyed Ross in amusement. "You passed out cold when the lash began to curl about your back, mister. You couldn't have lied if you had wanted to."

Ross reddened. "Well, it had been a long ride from Gran Morelos. I had to walk damned near half the distance."

"No offense. Better men than both of us have passed out beneath the lash. At least they didn't use a red-hot iron on your eyes. Colonel Melgosa has a fancy for Yaqui trackers. When he wants to find out something he lets those Yaquis practice a little on a prisoner. Before God, amigo, they could make a dumb man talk."

Ross felt a worm of uneasiness in his pinched gut. "You didn't tell me who *you* are. You seem to know all about me."

The man thrust out a lean hand. "My folks christened me Polk Desriders. Ain't that a handle to carry through life?"

Ross grinned as he gripped the hand. It was surprisingly strong. "What do they call you for short?"

"Des," said the man. "You a Texas man, Starkey?"

Ross shook his head. "New Mexico. Canadian River country." He narrowed his eyes. "Desriders? You got a brother about your age?"

Desriders shook his head.

"A cousin maybe?"

Desriders waved a hand. "By the peck," he said.

Ross took another drink. "One of them the Tascosa Kid?"

"No."

Ross wiped his mouth with the back of a dirty hand. "Now it's you who is lying like hell."

The gray eyes became cold for a fraction of a second. The

uneasiness came over Ross again. "By God," he said softly.
"It can't be *you*! The Kid was killed along the border two
years ago."

"No," said Desriders quietly.

Ross slowly took a cigarette from the limp pack and
lighted it, never taking his eyes from the man. Ross had ridden the Canadian, the Pecos and the Cimarron Rivers in his
cowpunching days, and although he had heard plenty about
the Tascosa Kid, he had never crossed his trail; nothing but
the trail of his record and reputation. They said that if the
Kid had notched his gun handles he would have whittled away
the walnut to the metal frames of the butts.

Desriders stood up and walked to the window, his spurs
jingling musically. "When Melgosa gets back, maybe tonight,
I might end up beside you against that wall."

"What's the charge against you, Des?"

"You can call me Tascosa. I dropped the 'Kid' when I got
across the border two years ago, two jumps and a holler ahead
of the sheriff of Verde County."

"That was a murder charge, wasn't it?"

Desriders nodded.

Ross blew a smoke ring. "If that's what's keeping you in
Mexico, you can go back," he said casually. "The charge was
suddenly dropped. Seems as though you've got some friends
in New Mexico."

Desriders turned slowly. "I don't like joshing," he said
coldly.

Ross looked around the filthy cell. "Who'd josh in a privy
like this? I'm tellin' you the truth, Kid."

Desriders narrowed his eyes. "By God," he said. "When did
that happen?"

"Three, four months ago."

"You're sure?"

"Positive."

Desriders ground a fist into the palm of his other hand.
"Cuerpo de Cristo! I never knew!" He looked at Ross.
"We've got to blow this *juzgado,* Starkey."

Ross spat into a corner. "Sure, Kid. Sure . . . any time.
Wake me when you're ready to go."

Desriders gripped Ross by the front of his filthy shirt.
"By God," he said between his teeth. "I mean it!"

"What have they got you in here for?" said Ross.

Tascosa released Ross' shirt. He grinned. "They caught me coming out of the bedroom window of the alcalde's daughter about dawn."

"Great," murmured Ross. "With all the *putas* in El Corralitos you have to have your fun in the mayor's daughter's bed."

Tascosa shook his head. "I was with his *wife,* not his daughter."

Ross waved a hand. "Well, pardon me all to hell! That's different!"

Tascosa flipped his cigarette between the bars. "You might as well know the mayor is Colonel Melgosa's brother. The mayor hasn't got the guts to try to kill me, and besides, he's more afraid of his wife than he is of me. It's a different matter with Colonel Melgosa."

"You don't have to remind me," murmured Ross.

Tascosa sat down and lighted a cigarette. "I've got a few friends in El Corralitos." He looked at Ross over the flare of the match. "That's how I came in here with the brandy and the cigarettes, and managed to keep these fancy Mex duds."

"If you're lying again," said Ross, "don't stop. You're tickling me all to hell, amigo."

Tascosa fanned out the match flame. "I knew as soon as I saw your loving kindness to that drowning cockroach you were the kind of man I could do business with."

Ross spread out his hands. "The shop is open, Tascosa. Shoot! You shoot with the mouth or Melgosa and his boys shoot with the rolling block Remingtons. Those softnosed .56-caliber slugs can cut a man in half and I ain't et enough in the past few days to have much of a middle. I'm open for any kind of proposition, Kid."

Tascosa walked to the door and listened for a while. He came close to Ross, wrinkling his nose. "Jesus," he murmured. "They ought to bury you right now."

Ross took a slug of brandy. "Be careful. I'm downright sensitive about such matters."

Tascosa placed his lips close to Ross' left ear. "Like I said: I've got friends. I know too much for them to let me start talking if Melgosa gets to work on me. You feel well enough to make a break?"

"You can try me," said Ross.

"I wouldn't leave a sick pup in this privy," said Tascosa. *"Escuche!* There won't be a moon tonight. The jailer will be occupied." Tascosa felt inside his left boot and drew out a file. "Those bars are too tough to break and this file ought to cut through them like a hot knife through butter."

"Great," murmured Ross. "What do we do then? Carry each other by turns piggyback two hundred miles to the border?"

"You open your mouth and just say anything, don't you? No thinking, no sense, just words, words, words!"

"It's a failing amongst my many virtues," said Ross modestly. He nipped at the flask again. The world was a little more pleasant.

"Lay off the *aguardiente* for a while! Look, I'm giving you a break. Melgosa might let you live one more night. You know as well as I do he won't fool with you when he gets back."

Ross was suddenly fully sober. He closed the flask cap.

"My friends have hidden a horse for me in an arroyo north of town. I can see to it that they put another one with it. Water, food, rifles and six-guns. I'll tell you one thing, hombre: You'd better be able to keep up, for this boy is heading for the border faster than lightning and eleven claps of thunder. If you can't keep up . . ."

Ross nodded. He looked up into the handsome face of the gunman. "Why bother with me at all?"

"I said I wouldn't leave a sick pup in here, didn't I?"

Ross nodded. "It's more than that," he said.

"All right! All right! Two gunfighters are better than one. Two good gunfighters can stand off a score of these greasers. Besides, we've got Apache country to pass through."

"What do you know about me?"

Tascosa smiled. "Zaldivar didn't hire you to *talk* gunfighting. I knew Zaldivar. Are you in on this, or do I go alone?"

"Try to get out of here without me," said Ross.

Tascosa nodded. He walked to the window and whistled softly. In a moment the admiring face of a young Mexican boy was at the window. "Juanito," said Tascosa with a winning smile. "Go to my friend and tell him he must have another horse placed with the one that is waiting. There must be another rifle and a pistol, with plenty of cartridges. You understand?"

The boy vanished as quickly as he had appeared.

"Can you trust him?" said Ross.

Tascosa grinned. "He loves me," he said.

"I wonder why?"

The Kid opened and then closed his mouth. "Tell me what you know about the country north of here," he said.

Later, when dusk came, Ross stayed near the cell door, listening to the sound of voices coming from the guardroom, while Tascosa worked on the rusted bars. There was a woman with the jailer. Another of Tascosa's *friends*, no doubt. She was keeping the jailer busy, from the sounds of drunken laughter. There was enough noise to cover the steady wheet-wheet-wheet of the sharp file as it bit into the iron. There were no other prisoners in the *calabozo*. Melgosa didn't throw his ordinary prisoners in there. The mission wall was too handy, and as Tascosa had said: "God will sort the souls."

It was very dark, both outside and in the guardroom, when Tascosa cut through the last bar. The jailer was either too busy with the woman to bother with his prisoners, or else he was dead drunk.

It was getting late, very close to midnight. The town was quiet except for the faint sound of guitar music coming from one of the cantinas on the *placita*.

Tascosa stood up on the cell stool and dropped a long leg outside, cursing softly as a bar stub gored his crotch. He slid to the ground and looked both ways. He whistled softly.

Ross looked around the dark hole of a cell for the last time, or so he hoped, then clambered outside. Tascosa handed him the flask. Ross drank deeply to gain temporary strength. His legs felt weak.

Tascosa bent and removed his chihuahua spurs, stuffing them into a pocket. He walked swiftly toward the dark bulk of the mission. Ross hurried after him, staggering now and then in his weakness. He remembered all too well what Tascosa had said: "I'll tell you one thing, hombre: You'd better be able to keep up, for this boy is heading for the border faster than lightning and eleven claps of thunder. *If you can't keep up . . .*"

Tascosa paused in the shelter of the mission wall. Ross leaned against the wall. He could vaguely see the dark marks where blood from shattered bodies had stained the scabrous wall.

"We'll cut through the cemetery," said Tascosa. He grinned. "You ain't afraid of ghosts, are you, hombre?"

Ross shook his head. "I'm more afraid of being made into one than of seeing one."

Tascosa slipped between the half-open rusted gates that led into the long-abandoned cemetery. Ross felt the night breeze sweeping from the north, drying the cold sweat on his face. The breeze smelled of freedom; of the border; of the United States. God, how good it felt!

The mission bell murmured softly as the breeze crept through the bell tower. The last time Ross had heard that ancient bell ring had been when a bullet had ricochetted from the wall below, after missing one of the *revolucionarios,* and had glanced from the bell high above the slaughter.

Tascosa was far ahead, striding toward the far gate that opened onto the edge of the desert that crept close to El Corralitos from the north. He turned to look back.

"Halt!" grated a harsh voice from beyond the wall. A gun hammer snicked back.

Tascosa turned slowly, raising his lean hands.

Ross faded back between the freshly mounded graves of his former comrades in the forces of Liberty. He darted clumsily into the thicker shadows of the wall, then slid between the rusted gates. There was no one in the area between him and the jail. He ran toward the west end of the mission. There was a chance they did not know he had been with Tascosa. There was a chance he could find the horses, food and water, and the guns, and head north by himself. He knew he'd rather die than go back to that privy of a jail.

He rounded the rear of the mission, stumbling over fallen tiles, cursing himself for his clumsiness. He faded into the thick cluster of thorny brush that had taken seed in a wall angle and had snuggled up along the old wall, stretching almost to the gate where Tascosa had been captured. Ross could hear the faint sound of voices, carried to him on the desert wind.

He leaned against the wall and fumbled for the flask. He drank deeply, draining the good brandy to get strength into his shaking legs, and as he did so, he seemed to see the handsome face of Tascosa looking at him from the darkness, although he knew the man was fifty yards away, facing a cocked rifle. If the sentry cried out, or fired, he'd waken the whole town, and gone would be Ross Starkey's precious dream of freedom.

"I wouldn't leave a sick pup in this privy," the Kid had said.

Ross knew it was now or never. Any minute Tascosa would be marched back to the jail and that would be the end of him when Melgosa got back. Maybe Melgosa *was* back. God help Tascosa if that was so.

"Look," Tascosa had said. "I'm giving you a break. Melgosa might let you live one more night. You know as well as I do he won't fool with you when he gets back."

The breeze rustled the brush. Freedom, thought Ross. Freedom in a five-minute walk to that arroyo and those horses.

"I said I wouldn't leave a sick pup in here, didn't I?" Tascosa had said.

Ross slipped the flask inside his shirt. He picked up a fallen broken tile and padded along the wall, as silent as a cat. He saw the big hat of the soldier, and his narrow shoulders. He was facing Tascosa. The breeze picked up, rustling the brush. Ross raised the tile and struck heavily. The sentry grunted and went down, while Tascosa neatly plucked the long-barreled Remington from his nerveless hands. He turned to look toward the town. The rifle struck the wall and the hammer sear slipped. The big .56-caliber cartridge exploded. The muzzle flash lighted the taut face of the sentry and his staring eyes. His neck was twisted at an unnatural angle. The roaring echo of the shot fled along the mission wall and rolled out into the desert.

"*Vamonos!*" cried Tascosa. He ran out into the desert, trailing the rifle.

The game was up, thought Ross as he staggered weakly after Tascosa. He made it five hundred yards from the mission and then went down. He looked back at El Corralitos. Lights were flashing on in the buildings. Lights bobbed about as men ran with lanterns in their hands. Horses whinnied in the corrals. Dogs barked.

He looked north. There was no sight or sound of Tascosa. Serves me right, thought Ross. I had freedom in my dirty hands and I had to let my head get soft. Now it's Tascosa riding north and me lying here waiting for Melgosa. When they find that dead sentry it'll be worse than a death sentence for me. Death would be preferable to what they will do.

CHAPTER TWO

THE HUNTERS were getting closer. Some of them were riding, while others led their horses as they searched through the thorny brush and in the shallow draws.

Ross bellied into a hollow. No gun, no horse; not even a shot of brandy to keep up his fast-waning courage.

Something hard struck a rock fifty feet from Ross. He turned, feeling for a weapon. He gripped a wedge-shaped rock.

A man whistled. "Hombre?" he called.

Ross closed his eyes. Weakness poured through him. It was Tascosa. "Here, Kid!" he said.

Tascosa came quickly through the darkness. He bent and picked up Ross, slinging him over his surprisingly broad shoulders. A hundred yards away a group of horsemen moved toward the two Americans. Tascosa walked steadily to the north, keeping the scant brush between him and the searching Mexicans.

It seemed like an hour before Ross smelled the horses. One of them whinnied. Tascosa heaved Ross up into the saddle. "Hang on," he said.

Ross felt a rifle in the saddle scabbard. A gunbelt, the loops full of cartridges and the holster heavy with a six-gun, hung around the big pie-plate pommel of the Mex saddle.

"I can't ride for you, hombre," said Tascosa.

"Lead out," said Ross. They'd never get him alive and he'd take a few with him, if he could see them through his onrushing fever. He looked back over his shoulder. A pinpoint of light showed as a soldier lighted a cigarette, the flare of the match revealing his bronzed face and thick mustache.

Tascosa led the way, deeper into the arroyo, cursing softly

as hoofs struck rocks embedded in the harsh ground. The wind moaned over the top of the arroyo.

Tascosa urged his horse up the arroyo side and waited for Ross. He pulled a bottle from a saddlebag and handed it to Ross. Ross pulled the cork with his teeth and swilled the booze. It was a shock. He had expected brandy. It was pulque, bitter and biting, but he felt strength pour into him. *"Salud,"* he said gaily to Tascosa as he drove the cork back into the bottle.

"Nothing like a damned fool for a *compañero* on a ride like this," said Tascosa.

They rode on into the windy darkness.

Farther and farther behind them the sounds of the searchers died away.

There was little other sound than the creak and rustle of leather and the steady thudding of the hoofs on the harsh desert surface. Now and then there was the soft pop of a cork to add to the other sounds.

Ross Starkey opened his eyes and instantly regretted it. The bright sunlight lanced into his eyes and penetrated deep into his brain, sickening him. He was half in and half out of the booze, with a fever added to it. He lay on a blanket within ten feet of a shallow *tinaja*. The dry wind made little ripples on the surface of the water in the rock pan. Ross closed his eyes, oblivious to everything else. The faint, tinkling sound of the water was all he could hear, or *wanted* to hear. He crawled from the blanket, wincing as the heat of the naked rock burned up through his thin trousers and shirt. He bellied inch by inch across the torturing surface of the ground until he could plunge his burning head into the water.

He raised his head, licking at the water that ran down his face, then plunged his head again into the cooling waters. At last he backed off and lay quietly, throbbing head resting on his wet forearms. He was sick, as deathly sick as he had ever been in his whole life. The sun swiftly dried the damp clothing and began to burn through the thin shirt, searing into the half-healed welts on his back. He was too weak to move.

The world seemed to reel and whirl about him. He didn't know where he was and he really didn't care. The last thing he remembered was forking a horse in the darkness of night and riding north, with the night wind fanning his fevered face. There had been a bottle. He vaguely remembered emptying it and then heaving it as far as he could, hearing it crash on the hard ground, laughing uproariously while some-one tried to stop him.

Ross raised his head. "Tascosa!" he said hoarsely.

"You called?" the polite voice said from above him.

Ross looked up. Tascosa was squatting on a rock ledge twenty feet above him, a rifle across his thighs, a cigarette dangling from his lips, a faint wraith of smoke about his lean, bronzed face.

Ross sat up, wincing in agony. *"Por amor de Dios,"* he groaned.

Tascosa spat. "There's another bottle beside your blanket," he said coldly. "You look as though you need some of it. *Some*, I said, hombre!" There was a quiet warning in his voice.

Ross crawled like a whipped hound to the bottle, pulled the cork with his teeth and drank deeply. He wiped his cracked lips with the back of a dirty hand and looked up at Tascosa with a sickly grin. "Least you could'a done," he said, "was keep it out'a the sun. Burns like cougar piss."

Tascosa flipped away the cigarette and began to roll an-other. "I'll have a bucket of cracked ice sent down," he said dryly.

Ross tipped the bottle up again. He drank deeply again and then once more, than placed the cork in the bottle. For a few minutes the harsh booze hurt like the devil and then the alcohol set to work and a dullness came over the throbbing pain in his head. "Where are we?" he said.

"Just north of the Rio de Haros."

Ross digested that. "A little far west, ain't we?"

Tascosa lighted his fresh cigarette. "Maybe. Eat some grub. I don't want to sit here all day. It's late enough as it is."

"I ain't hungry."

Tascosa looked down at the older man. "The grub is in that saddlebag," he said flatly. "Eat, gawddammit! You're weak enough as it is!"

Ross stood up, his eyes blazing. "You can pull leather out'a here any time you like," he said.

Their eyes clashed and neither man looked away. Tascosa

blew smoke out of his nostrils. "Forget it," he said quietly.
"We're both on edge. It wasn't no picnic riding all last night
with you, hombre. Between the fever and the booze you
were out of this world, I tell you."

Ross nodded. "I guess you're right," he said quietly. "I
apologize, amigo."

"Forget it, I said! If it hadn't been for you back at the
mission I'd likely be dead by now. I don't forget those things,
Ross."

Ross ate quickly, forcing down the dry food, but admitting
to himself that Tascosa was right. Between the water, the
booze and the food he felt a little better, but his legs were
rubbery and he knew he had a day or two of hell in front
of him. He'd have to make it. There was no going back now,
or waiting for the *Federalistas* to catch up.

"How does it look?" said Ross.

Tascosa shrugged. "Saw a little dust a while back. Couldn't
tell if it was a dust devil or not. You ready?"

"Any time."

Ross got the horses. He filled the canteens and drank
deeply once more from the *tinaja*. He nipped at the bottle
before Tascosa reached the flat ground, then slid the bottle
into one of his saddlebags. The booze headache was sufficiently dulled to enable him to ride.

Tascosa led the way through a shallow, winding canyon.
The area was as deserted as though they were riding on the
moon. It was deathly hot and the thin dust rose from the
harsh ground to coat both horse and man. Now and then
Tascosa looked back at Ross, riding with bent head, one
hand gripping the pie-plate pommel. If they had to move in a
hurry Ross would never make it. Tascosa prayed for darkness.
There would be a new moon that night. They could rest in
the pre-moon darkness, then ride all night toward the border.

Both of them slept like the dead, heedless of anyone approaching their camp through the thick darkness, until the
first faint rays of the moon appeared over the mountains far
west of the distant Chihuahua Road. Ross felt better as they
rode under the light of the rising moon. Now and then he
looked about him. Tascosa was leading the way, as he had
done ever since they had left El Corralitos, but he was riding too far west, slanting away from the easier ground east of
the Sierra Vallecillos. Ross didn't give a damn. All he wanted

to do was reach the border and sleep for a week. Still . . .
Ross wondered about Tascosa. They should be making a bee-
line for the border, not slanting off the trail.

The moon was fully up when Tascosa turned in his saddle.
"How far is it from here?" he said quietly.

"How far is what?" asked Ross.

"The spring."

"What spring?"

Tascosa leaned forward in his saddle. "The Eye of God,"
he said.

Ross rubbed his bristly jaws. "I've heard of the place," he
said. "We're too far west for it."

Tascosa felt for the makings. He rolled a cigarette, watching Ross all the while. He tossed the makings to Ross.

"We're wasting time sitting here," said Ross.

"No we ain't," corrected Tascosa.

"There's no profit in riding all this way, then sitting here
waiting for them to catch up."

Tascosa snapped a lucifer on his thumbnail and lighted up,
his amused eyes on Ross. "There *is* a profit near The Eye of
God," he said quietly.

Ross' hands stopped in the act of rolling a cigarette. "Meaning?" he said.

"Five thousand in gold," said Tascosa.

Ross casually finished rolling the cigarette. He lighted it,
fanned out the match, then looked at his companion. "Now
it's you that has the fever," he said.

"Zaldivar's gold cache," said Tascosa. "You see, hombre,
you did a helluva lot of talking last night. Too *much* maybe.
You lied beautifully back in that *calabozo*. You almost had
me convinced."

Ross grinned. "No gold cached at The Eye of God," he
said. "Just repeating rifles. Henrys and Spencers. Too heavy
to haul away."

Tascosa blew a smoke ring. "Well, anyways, we'll take a
look-see," he said.

Ross shrugged. "Keno."

"Come ride up here beside me, hombre. It gets lonely."

Ross touched the sorrel with his heels and rode up beside
the younger man. "Waste of time," he growled.

"Just show me the way, hombre." Tascosa smiled sweetly.
"We have to water the *caballos* anyway."

Ross led the way up the twisted canyon that branched east of the mountains to end in a jumbled tangle of rock and thorny brush. He looked back at Tascosa. "The 'Paches like to lie around here waiting for white men who come to water their horses," he said.

"Do tell," said Tascosa politely.

Ross held out his hands, palms upward. He slid his rifle from its scabbard and placed it across his thighs.

The moonlight shone down into the canyon, glinting from the silvery surface of the spring that welled out from beneath a huge overhanging rock face, whiskered with thorny brush and scrub trees that clung tenaciously to the rock face, their roots buried in shallow soil pockets.

Ross watered his sorrel, watching Tascosa out of the corners of his eyes. Tascosa was completely at ease. He sang softly in Spanish as he watered his black.

"Take it easy," said Ross. "You're making too much noise. Damned 'Paches and Yaquis can hear like dogs."

Tascosa leaned against his horse and rolled a cigarette. "No problem," he said. "They won't come near this place."

"Why?"

"It's taboo for them. Some kind of curse because of the dead men buried here who are said to walk on moonlit nights."

"You know a helluva lot, don't you?" sneered Ross.

"Sí," said Tascosa complacently.

"Where'd you learn that whopper?"

Tascosa ran the cigarette paper along his tongue tip and folded it over. He thrust it into his mouth and felt for a match. "Why," he said, "friend of mine told me."

"He didn't know from nothing."

Tascosa smiled as he lighted the cigarette. "I wouldn't put it that way."

"Who told you?" demanded Ross.

Tascosa blew out a cloud of smoke. "You did," he said. "Like I told you: You did a lot of talking last night."

Ross grinned. "Keno," he said. "You hold all the aces."

"Where's the gold?"

Ross tethered the sorrel to a scrub tree and took his rifle. He walked up the rock-littered slope until he reached a level area, ringed by upright boulders. "Here," he said.

"Show me," said Tascosa.

Ross leaned his rifle against a rock and began to pull brush away from a crevice. He looked carefully for rattlesnake sign and then he dragged out a heavy wooden box which he placed on a flat rock. Weakness poured through him as he exerted himself.

"Open it," said Tascosa.

Ross turned, his mouth opening in defiance. He closed his mouth. Tascosa held a cocked six-gun in his hand and his cold gray eyes probed into Ross' eyes. Ross worked at the thumbscrews. He pulled off the lid of the box. The moonlight shone dully on the coins.

"Dios en cielo!" gasped Tascosa. "Is that all of it?"

Ross shook his head. "Three more like it are hidden all around here."

"Get 'em!" snapped Tascosa.

Ross folded his arms. "Find 'em yourself," he said quietly. "No use in waving that cutter. You kill me and you won't ever find any of them. This was the easy one, hombre."

"Find 'em, damn you!"

Ross grinned. "Look behind you," he said. "Down in the canyon."

"You think I'm a kid to be taken in like that?"

"Look, you bastard!" said Ross.

Tascosa turned and shot a glance down into the canyon, then he turned again to Ross. He opened, then closed his mouth, then turned again to look down into the canyon. "Jesus Christ!" he said.

Ross laughed softly. "Hellsfire, Kid! There are only a round dozen of them. 'Course, there's no telling how *many* of 'em are still down in the canyon."

Tascosa turned and his face was as set and taut as a death mask, and for the first time Ross felt the cold chill of murder emanating from the man. "You bastard," he said thinly. "You said they wouldn't come here! That it had a curse on it. You lied even in your delirium!"

Ross nodded. "I'm ashamed of myself," he said. "Mother always said I'd come to no good end."

"What can we do!" Tascosa's voice rose to a high pitch. He would have faced a dozen Mexicans or Americans, one man against them all, but a dozen Apaches can unnerve even the toughest of hardcases.

Ross picked up the box and dropped it into the crevice. He

pushed the brush back atop it, then looked at Tascosa.
"They won't touch it," he said.

"What about us?"

Ross picked up his rifle. The Apaches were out of sight,
hidden behind broken ground. "They like to ambush," he
said quietly. "They don't like to be ambushed. They figure on
two white men sitting down at The Eye of God, filling their
dry guts with water, only *we* ain't going to be there. Get
your rifle. Jump!"

Tascosa wasted no time in sliding down to his horse, with
Ross laughing softly as he came down behind him. Despite
Ross' own icy fear, he couldn't help but laugh at the change
in Tascosa.

They led the horses into a dead-end gully, then padded,
Tascosa spurless, through the brush until they reached a
ledge that ran along the canyon wall. Ross dropped to his
belly and peered between two rocks. "Take a look," he whispered.

Tascosa crawled up beside Ross. He could see eight of
the warriors riding slowly toward the spring, and yet their
horses made no sound.

"Rawhide boots on the *caballos*," said Ross. He levered a
round of .44/40 into the chamber of the repeater. He looked
at Tascosa. "I'll start from the rear, and you start from the
front. I'll try to meet you in the middle."

Tascosa grinned. "First one to get five gets first crack at
the other three, wherever the hell they are."

Two rifle barrels poked between rocks. The moonlight
made the night almost as bright as day. One of the horses at
the spring whinnied. The first Apache drew in his paint pony
and leaned forward, holding up a hand to stop his companions. At that instant Tascosa fired, to be instantly echoed
by Ross' first shot. The canyon became a hell of crashing
explosions, intermingled with the roaring echoes slamming
back and forth between the canyon walls, overpowering
the screams of the Apaches. In three minutes thirty murderous
rounds of softnosed .44/40 slugs had ripped all life from
the bucks and had killed three horses, while the others galloped madly off in all directions, crashing through the thorny
brush.

Acrid gunsmoke mingled with the smell of hot brass. Ross
wiped his sweating face as he fed bright brass cartridges into

the magazine of the hot, smoking Winchester. "Let's get to
hell out'a here," he said. "Those four who are left won't
bother us—for a time at least. But I'll guarantee you, if
there are any more of them within fifty miles of here, they'll
be on our asses by dawn tomorrow."

They scrambled back to their horses. "What about the
gold?" said Tascosa as he swung up on his black.

Ross grinned. "You want to go back for it, hombre? Go
ahead. I'll see you in Lordsburg when you get there. You
can stake me to a meal, a bottle, a poker game and a
woman."

Tascosa cursed bitterly as Ross led the way through the
pathless tangle. Ross grinned again and again, and it wasn't
the occasional shot of red-eye he took to keep him going that
made him grin. At that, it had been a near thing. . . .

CHAPTER THREE

YOU PAY A PRICE for everything. Maybe at the time of purchase, or perhaps years later, when you least expect it. But you always pay the price. The thought was Ross Starkey's as he felt the sorrel stagger under him. The sorrel was weakening fast, but not much faster than his rider. Fear, booze and desperation had driven Ross from the place where he had been awaiting execution. There had been no hope for him there. But he had left one desperate situation for another. They had outdistanced or lost the *Federalistas,* but both of them knew they had not outdistanced or lost the Apaches. There was no sight nor sound of them in the two days that had passed since they had ambushed the party at The Eye of God, but that meant nothing. An Apache is not seen unless he *wants* to be seen.

Ross' last great effort had been the killing of the bucks and the swift ride on tired horses out of the canyon, heading into the malpais country north of the Sierra Vallecillos. There was likely no water there, and there was none in the canteens. The wind came fitfully and when it did come it did nothing but stir up the bitter dust that scoured the throat and burned the eyes.

"We had to kill them," said Ross.

"Sure, sure," said Tascosa bitterly. "We kill eight of them and bring down half a hundred. By God, you tricked me! I'd never have gone to The Eye of God if it hadn't been for you!"

Ross spat dryly. He swayed in the saddle. Fever, heat and lack of water were slowly destroying him.

"Five thousand in gold lying there!" said Tascosa. "Five thousand! And we can't get at it."

We, thought Ross. He remembered all too well the look on

28

Tascosa's face and the cocked pistol in his hand when he had seen Ross pull out the first box of gold.

There was a low line of hills ahead of them, shimmering and moving in the heat haze. Beyond them showed the humped shapes of leaden-colored, hairless mountains. Beyond those mountains should be the border, but that wouldn't make any difference to the Apaches. They owed allegiance to no country; to no one but themselves.

Ross turned in his saddle. Here and there dust devils swirled lazily across the baking plain.

"Serve you right if I left you behind for those bushy-headed devils," said Tascosa.

Ross rode on. He did not look up. The hills always seemed to recede like waves on a shore every time he looked at them.

The sun was low in the west when they reached the hills. The country behind them was still empty of life and yet there was an uneasiness in the leaden air. A hostile, alien feeling came from the land.

They found the shallow *tinaja* in a silent, brooding canyon that slashed through the hills like an open saber wound. They pushed aside the floating scum and pinkish bladders and strained the gamey water through their dirty scarves. There was enough to water the horses, fill their own bellies and the canteens, but hardly a drop more.

Tascosa rolled a cigarette. "That sorrel is about done," he said.

Ross nodded. He wiped his cracked lips. The sun was almost gone but the heat of it hung over the windless land, enervating and weakening, waiting for its insensate chance to kill. The black was tired, but it had reserves of strength the sorrel had lacked.

"We can rest here awhile," said Tascosa.

Ross did not answer. He picked up his rifle and staggered a little as he climbed a slope. He looked south, then west and east.

"What is it?" called Tascosa.

Ross did not answer. He pointed with his rifle. A thin streamer of smoke seemed pasted against the clear western sky like coarse hair on pale blue cloth. It was about five miles off.

"Ranch burning?" said Tascosa.

Ross shook his head.

"Campfire?"

Ross leaned on his rifle, almost utterly spent. "They're gathering over there," he said. "By moonrise they'll have bucks ahead of us, between us and the border."

"We can head east."

Ross shook his head. "They'll have scouts that way. If we get spotted, those scouts will signal the main party. Besides, even if we could get past them, we could run into the *Federalistas*."

Tascosa blew a smoke ring. "We can't go south."

"We can't stay here."

Tascosa looked at the brown sorrel. The horse stood with spraddled legs, head hanging, yellowish foam drying on its gummy lips, its sides heaving erratically.

Tascosa didn't have to say what he was thinking. The black was in good condition. Good for fifty more miles at least.

Ross clambered down the rocks and felt for the makings. He rolled and lighted a cigarette.

"We can't hole up here," said Tascosa. "No water."

"The Apaches will have every water hole north of here covered by dawn."

Tascosa looked sideways at Ross. "Hell of a note, ain't it?"

Ross nodded. His head was throbbing from the exertion of climbing. If the sorrel died Ross could hardly walk five miles, maybe less.

"Let's go," said Tascosa. He mounted the black and rode away from the dry *tinaja*.

A gecko lizard looked at Ross with bright eyes, then scuttled away, diving into cover in a slit of rock so narrow it seemed impossible for him to fit in it.

"Little ol' lizard," said Ross, as he mounted, "you got us humans beat three ways from Sunday."

The sun died in a welter of rose and gold and a faint dry breeze came whispering across the darkened desert and crept into the broken hills.

The sorrel went down for good just at the edge of the looming mountains. Ross just cleared the leather as the horse fell. He drew his rifle from the scabbard and unhooked the big canteen. He took the last bottle from the saddlebag and thrust it inside his filthy shirt. He looked about. The darkness was soft and velvety, but it had a menacing quality to it. There was no sign nor sound of Tascosa and the black. A faint wash of moonlight stained the eastern sky. *By moonrise they'll have bucks ahead of us, between us and the border.* Those were Ross' own words.

He walked unsteadily through the clinging darkness, feeling the hot rock burn up through his worn rope sandals. All he wanted was a chance to put the rifle muzzle into his mouth and pull the trigger before the swift, silent rush of the bucks.

The eastern mountains etched their craggy tops against the rising moonlight. The wind shifted, rustling the dry brush, making dust eddies that swirled up the plodding man and stung his eyes. He coughed.

The moonlight touched the dull mountains ahead of Ross and began to work its alchemy on the colorless slopes. The higher elevations began to stand out in the silvery light, but it only served to deeply accentuate the pools of shadow on the rough slopes. What was hiding in those stygian shadows?

There was a foreboding silence about the night. Memories came back to Ross Starkey as he plodded along, one aching foot in front of the other, on and on, and there was no ending. He remembered the little *ranchita* on the Canadian where he had been born. His brother still owned it, although none of the Starkeys now lived on it. Lloyd Starkey had gone and got himself educated for the law and now practiced in Santa Fe. Last rumor Ross had heard of him, he had been working his way into Territory politics. Maybe if Ross got out of this scrape he'd con Lloyd into letting him run the *ranchita.* He laughed shortly. There was enough gold back at The Eye of God to buy the *ranchita* and a couple more like it.

He stumbled and went down on one knee, wincing in pain. When he got to his feet and started walking again he had to limp, favoring the badly bruised knee. "Damned near thirty years old," he said to the night, "and not enough sense to come in out'a the rain." He felt his cracked lips, then sipped a little water, spitting it back into the canteen. "I wonder where Mary Ellen Spragg is now?" He grinned. "Probably fatter than she was, and got a brood of kids." He shook his head. "She was sure sweet on ol' Ross." He pulled out the almost empty bottle of booze. "Might'a made a good wife at that. How about that, booze bottle? You got any answers in that glass belly of yourn?"

He emptied the bottle, gathering temporary strength from the biting, pungent pulque. He carefully placed the bottle on a rock and walked on, looking back to see the moonlight glistening on it, standing there like a fat-bellied knight in armor. Just another dead soldier. "I wonder how many of them I've killed in the past ten years?" said Ross. "Damned near thirty years old and not a damned bit of sense."

His leg throbbed and each step became agonizing, while each time he slid on a glazed pebble, or hit a shallow dip in the ground, a lance of sheer torture shot through it.

The moon was fully up when he reached the canyon mouth. The wind whispered through it. He had no desire to walk into it, but he'd never be able to walk around it. Apaches knew the white man's ways. Apaches kept to the heights, never the low ground unless it was absolutely unavoidable. White men as a rule kept to the low ground. Ross had no choice this night of hell.

He entered the brooding silence of the canyon, walking as softly as possible, but even so, his slightest noise brought an answering echo. The place was like a rock sound box.

The moon was grinning expectantly down into the canyon when Ross went down as the sorrel had gone down. He gripped his rifle with almost nerveless hands. If he wasn't seen in the moonlight, they'd find him in the darkness. They could hardly miss his ripe scent. Dawn would bring death in the form of thick-haired men walking silently on thick-soled desert moccasins, liquid eyes staring at him through masks of white bottom clay. There would be no expression on their faces as they slowly tortured him, keeping him alive as long as possible.

A horse blowed in the shadows.

Can't blame him, thought Ross. I'd blow too if I smelled me. He grinned, wincing as a new crack opened at the side of his mouth. He rested his head on the warm rock.

Feet husked on the harsh ground. They stopped.

Ross looked up into the set face of Tascosa. "I never thought you'd get this far," said Tascosa.

"Hitched me a ride on a moonbeam," cracked Ross. He closed his eyes.

"I can't leave you here . . . *alive*," said Tascosa.

Ross rested his pounding head on his forearms. "You can't shoot," he said. "The sound would carry for miles."

"I wasn't thinking of shooting."

"You've been down here long enough to know how to use a knife."

There was a long pause. Ross looked up. Tascosa was still standing there. "You silly sonofabitch," said Tascosa. "Don't you know when you're licked?"

Ross shook his head.

Tascosa squatted beside Ross and placed a hard hand on Ross' forehead. "Am I all right?" said Ross.

Tascosa picked up the rifle. "You won't need this," he said. "You got the six-gun."

"Take that too," said Ross. "You can hock it for ten bucks in Lordsburg."

Tascosa rubbed his whiskered face. He looked up at the moonlit sky, then down the long stretch of the empty canyon. "This place should be crotch-deep in Apaches by now," he said, almost as though to himself.

Ross couldn't help it. "Maybe they got a taboo on this place too. Hawww!"

"You sound just like a jackass I once knew," said Tascosa. "Relative of yours?"

Tascosa turned on a heel and vanished into the darkness.

Ross slowly eased out the Colt. He opened the loading gate and turned the cylinder. It was fully loaded.

Hoofs rang dully on the rock. Tascosa reappeared, leading the tired black. He bent down and lifted Ross, staggering a little with the load. He dumped Ross unceremoniously over the saddle. He carried the rifle in his hand as he led the black north up the empty canyon.

Ross awoke in thick darkness. He lay on a dusty blanket in a rocky area. He raised his head. The night was as quiet as a tomb. "Tascosa?" he said. There was no answer, not even a whinny from the black. Ross' feet were bare. The pistol lay on the blanket beside him and the rifle leaned against a rock. Ross forced himself to sit up. Why had Tascosa taken the worn rope sandals? His questing hand struck a boot and then another. He pulled them close. They were Tascosa's finely figured Mex boots. Ross rubbed his shaggy, dusty head. "Beats the hell out'a me," he said.

He crawled about the area, sensing rather than seeing that he was high on a slope that slanted down toward the east. The moon was fully gone.

Ross leaned back against a rock. His right knee was painfully swollen. He could go no further, and even if the knee had not been injured he knew well enough his strength was almost gone. There was just enough left to press trigger. Tascosa at least had left him that insurance against the slow, agonizing death meted out by Apaches.

He remembered the Sangre de Cristo Mountains and the cool, swift-rushing streams, as different from this lifeless land of baked rock as heaven is from hell. He remembered the timbered heights of the Capitans and the Sierra Blanca. He remembered a little *placita* there and a girl named Serafina. No, it had been Filomena. He might have married her except for his cursed Anglo-Saxon superiority. But then she would have started to become shapeless by now. Just as loving and dutiful as ever, but *fat*. How old had she been? Seventeen? No, it had been fifteen, marriageable age enough in that country. He might have married her at that except for her three brothers, tough as boots, who had ridden with the Seven Rivers corrida in those days, when Ross had been riding with the San Patricio corrida. There could have been no peace between them. That had been a long time ago. No, only seven years.

Now and then he peered down the dark slopes, seeing nothing, but listening well. He had to be ready with the pistol before the swift rush of painted death.

He slept. He didn't know how long. It had been a dreamless sleep, but it had refreshed him.

Something moved down the slope. Ross cocked the Colt. His cold sweat greased the gun butt. His breath came short and fast and he was certain it could be heard a good distance away.

A shadow moved. No, it was a man! Ross raised the pistol. Better to take along a few for honorary pallbearers before he used the last round on himself. Show them how a *white* man can die.

A soft, low whistle came up the slope.

Ross wet his cracked lips, darting his burning eyes back and forth, looking back over his shoulder for a sudden rush.

The whistle came again. "Ross?" called Tascosa.

Jesus God! Ross slumped against warm rock. He was completely unnerved. For a minute he thought he was going to faint.

Tascosa came up the slope leading three horses. One of them was the black. "You got guts enough to ride, hombre?" he said.

Ross looked down at Tascosa's feet. He was wearing Ross' thin rope sandals. As Tascosa led a horse to Ross, Ross thought the younger man was wearing black gloves. "Where'd you get them *caballos*?" asked Ross hoarsely.

Tascosa grinned. "The only place I could," he said.

"The Apaches?" said Ross incredulously.

Tascosa nodded. "Keno," he said.

"Impossible!" said Ross.

Tascosa looked at him wearily. "There were only two of them. One was a boy, an untried warrior, with the drinking tube and head-scratching stick hanging about his dirty neck. He was no problem. The buck was an old man, but he fought well enough, for a *buck*."

Ross looked at Tascosa's hands. He knew now what made them look so black.

Tascosa mounted one of the captured horses. "Mex Army saddles," he said casually. "The Apaches must have hit one of their patrols." He grinned. "Maybe one of the patrols looking for us. Dog eat dog."

"I still don't believe it," said Ross. He picked up his rifle and pulled himself weakly into the saddle, his breath coming harshly in his raw throat.

Tascosa looked at Ross from under the brim of his big Mex hat. "You said I had been down here long enough to learn how to use a knife. You were right, hombre." He touched the horse with his heels and rode down the slope, leading the worn black.

It was still a long way from the border.

CHAPTER FOUR

Ross Starkey sat on a chair, tilted back against the adobe wall behind him, in the shade of the *ramada* that had been built against the ranch house. A warm breeze swept across the open country and swung the water olla back and forth in its hangings. He slowly rolled a cigarette, watching the lone horseman pick his way across the broken ground north of the isolated ranch. A Winchester rested beside Ross' chair. Ross lighted the cigarette and watched the smoke swirl out into the slanting sunlight. It had been a week since Tascosa had left for Deming, leaving Ross in the care of Bass Orcutt and his Mexican wife. Tascosa had rested for some weeks before that, seemingly reluctant to leave the place, but at last he had gone, to find out if Ross had been right about Tascosa having been cleared of the murder charge held against him in Verde County. Somehow or other Ross had the idea that Tascosa didn't quite trust him. He grinned as he remembered the look on Tascosa's face when he had seen the Apaches closing in on The Eye of God.

Ross got to his feet. His knee was still a little sore, but it was healing fast. He must have gained five or six pounds in the past six weeks, with Consuelo Orcutt's good cooking in him. Consuelo was quite a dish herself, a long way from her native town in Sonora. Ross had never quite figured out how a spavined, weatherbeaten old hoss like Orcutt had gotten himself such a wife, and how he managed to keep her on his isolated ranch on the edge of Apache country, miles from any other people.

Ross picked up the rifle. It was a white man, and not a Mexican by the look of his clothing. They weren't so far over the border that a party of *Federalistas* couldn't slip over in the dark of the moon and snap up a couple of fugitives, then be gone by dawn. Ross levered a round into the rifle.

The horseman waved as he reached the sagging fence. "Put down that damned repeater!" he yelled. It was Tascosa all right.

Ross leaned the rifle against the wall. He watched Tascosa ride toward the house. He had done himself proud in his new rig-out. Dark gray hat and coat, white shirt and string tie. "You look like a circuit-riding preacher," said Ross. "Got a Bible in them saddlebags?"

Tascosa shook his head. "Better than that," he said. "Got some clothes for you and a bottle of rye or two."

"Christmas comes but once a year," said Ross.

Tascosa swung down and slapped the dust from his clothing.

"How was Deming?" said Ross.

Tascosa shrugged. "I went all the way to Las Cruces," he said.

"That's damned close to Verde County, Kid."

Tascosa looked about. "Dammit," he snapped. "I told you to call me Polk around here!"

Ross smiled. "They ain't here. Old Bass took his bride over to Columbus. She deviled him into it. Wanted a new dress and some other odds and ends. Seems like she's taking a new interest in life around here, now that you got a job with old Bass."

Tascosa spat. *"Had,"* he said. "You were right about me being cleared, Ross. I can go back home now."

"Where?" said Ross dryly.

Tascosa took the saddlebags from the black. "I got nothing against Verde County," he said.

Ross flipped away his cigarette butt and began to roll a fresh smoke. "Funny thing," he said slowly. "A dead man most always has relatives and friends."

"I said I was cleared!"

"Yeh," said Ross. He lighted the cigarette.

Tascosa looked at him, little white lines radiating from the corners of his mouth. "Sometimes you talk too much," he said coldly.

"Sometimes I don't talk enough," said Ross.

"That'll be the day!"

Ross shrugged. "I was doing some listening to old Bass the

other night. Might be to your advantage to listen to *him*, instead of talking to his wife all the time."

"Go on."

"Hand me one of them bottles first."

Tascosa handed Ross a bottle of the rye. Ross took a drink. He wiped his mouth. "Begod," he said. He gasped. "After old Bass' kill-or-cure booze, this is like manna."

Tascosa handed Ross a second bottle. "You mean nectar," he said. "Manna is a food."

"You been reading books again," said Ross. "Anyway, old Bass was doing a lot of talking while you were gone. Seems like you didn't fool him none with that Polk name of yours, even if it is right. He had a damned good idea who you were. Maybe he saw you working on his wife."

"You always run off at the mouth with a shot of booze in you," said Tascosa disgustedly.

"I'm making sense," said Ross. "Things ain't the same back in Verde County, Kid. Bass says they're choosing up sides again."

"Helluva lot that scrawny old tom turkey knows."

"He knows enough. Used to live thereabouts. Come out here because it was peaceful."

Tascosa laughed. "Peaceful? With Apaches looking over the next rise and *bandidos* riding over the border in the dark for a crack at the nearest Americano ranch?"

"He meant it was peaceful compared to Verde County. Here you can kill an Apache or a *bandido* and no one says anything except good riddance. But back in Verde County it's a *feud*, man! One killing follows another and you ain't exactly innocent, Kid."

Tascosa placed the saddlebags on the chair and pulled out some clothing which he tossed to Ross. He handed him a nice pair of secondhand boots. "Couldn't get any new ones your size, hombre. These'll do until we get someplace civilized."

"Like where?" said Ross.

Tascosa looked at him. "El Paso?"

"Fair enough. But I've got a job here."

Tascosa looked out over the barren land. "Here? You make me laugh. My old wounds hurt when I laugh like that."

"It'll do for a time," said Ross.

"Punching a handful of cows?"

"You got any better offers?" Ross quickly raised a hand. "Don't answer that!"

Tascosa rolled a smoke, leaning against a post, eyeing Ross from beneath the brim of his low-pulled hat. "I was figuring on heading north for a time. Maybe Albuquerque or Vegas."

"We'll need money."

"We can get it."

"How?" said Ross quietly.

The wind shifted and the rattlely-bang windmill began to whirr stridently into life.

"Punching cows?" prodded Ross.

Tascosa shot a hard look at him. "That ain't my line."

"It's good enough for me."

"You weren't exactly punching cows with Zaldivar," said Tascosa.

Ross sipped a little rye. "Only by the grace of God did I get out of that mess."

"And me," said Tascosa. "You'da never made it without me, hombre."

"Granted," said Ross. "But I'm damned near thirty years old. I don't aim to end up being a broken-down cowpoke sitting in a cantina talking about the 'old days' while I'm cadging drinks, and I don't want to die with my boots on."

"Like me, maybe?"

Ross lowered the bottle. "You don't *have* to go back to Verde County," he said quietly. "Or maybe you *do* have to."

"You don't make sense, as usual."

"They pay a lot for good gunfighters there. Enough to stake a man for a while, if he lives through it. I never did know if they guaranteed a real funeral, with candles and all that."

"Look, Ross," said the younger man. "Throw in with me. We can go to El Paso, or Albuquerque, or anywhere you like, for a time anyway. Then we can mosey quiet like into Verde County and get the feel of things. You can side me. I need a good partner. You and me could make a real team."

Ross carefully corked the bottle. He looked steadily at Tascosa. "You're a loner," he said. "Like me. Only I don't want to be a loner anymore. You want a reputation and I want one too, only they ain't quite the same."

"You're going respectable?" said Tascosa with a faint smile.

"I'm going to try."

"I can get you in with some big men in Verde County."

"I'll try it on my own," said Ross. "Somewheres else."

"This is goodbye then?"

"For a time, Kid. We'll meet again some day."

Tascosa nodded. He thrust out a hard hand. "I want to make it to Las Cruces by tomorrow morning," he said.

Ross took the proffered hand. "You can go in the morning," he said.

Tascosa did not answer. He walked into the bunkhouse and in a few minutes he was back with his gear, stuffed into a warbag. He slung the warbag over the rump of the black. "Keep the saddlebags," he said over his shoulder.

"I owe you something," said Ross.

Tascosa mounted and spurred the black. He rode toward the gate. "You don't owe me a damned thing," he said back over his shoulder.

Ross watched him ride to the northeast, raising a trailing wreath of thin dust, shot through with the dying light of the sun. A feeling of utter loneliness struck through Ross.

It wasn't until he was halfway through the first bottle of rye that he suddenly realized that Tascosa must be a helluva lot lonelier than he was, but there was a difference. Tascosa would never have admitted it to Christ himself.

He was still sitting there in the velvety darkness, looking up at the glittering ice-chip stars, when he heard the rattling of the ancient buckboard and the thudding of hoofs on the hard-packed road.

The buckboard was halted in front of the *ramada* and a lean, rawboned man swung awkwardly down to the ground. "Gawddammit, Ross," he said. "You could'a lit a lamp, or a candle or somethin'. Man comin' clear from them hills and not a light. Struck me maybe the 'Paches had come. You shouldn't ought'a done that, Ross."

"Bass," said Ross from the thick shadows. "Get lost!" He hiccupped.

Orcutt helped Consuelo down from the buckboard. The odor of cheap perfume, mingled with the bitter smell of the dust, drifted to Ross.

"You get some grub cookin', Connie," said Bass.

She looked toward Ross. "How many eating, Ross?" she said.

"Polk ain't here," said Ross.

"Not back yet?" demanded Bass. "If he's goin' to work for me he's got to be here! I got a good mind to send you after him!"

"Save the time and trouble," said Ross. He lighted the cigarette he had just rolled and the flare of the match revealed his lean hawk's face and bitter eyes. "He ain't never comin' back."

"How do you know this?" said Consuelo swiftly.

Ross fanned out the match. "He came back and left again."

Bass lifted a sack out of the buckboard. "Verde County, hey?"

"*Quién sabe?*" said Ross.

"They'll kill him yet. You mark my words."

"He can do a little killin' himself, Bass. Don't never forget that."

Ross got up and limped to the buckboard, watching Consuelo switch her rounded little outraged tail into the dark house. Ross took a box of groceries from the buckboard. "What's bothering Connie?" said Ross.

Bass grinned. "Well, we wasn't goin' to tell anybody . . . yet." He shifted his chew and spat accurately at a post. He wiped his juicy lips and grinned again, looking sideways at Ross.

Ross had an uneasy feeling. Damn that Tascosa anyway!

Bass hefted the sack across his narrow shoulders. "By God," he said, almost breathlessly. "Here I was about to think she wasn't goin' to breed. Did my damnedest, I tell you, Ross, and I was quite a rooster with the ladies back in Verde County, I tell you."

"*Muy hombre,*" said Ross.

"Well, the doc says there ain't any doubt now. You and Tascosa brought me luck, I tell you."

Ross started for the house. "Brought you more than just luck," he said in a low voice.

"What's that, amigo?" said Bass.

"I'm glad we brought you luck," said Ross. He shrugged. You needed it, he thought, but not quite the way you figured it.

Later, at supper, with the guttering lamplight playing on the faded and yellowing plaster of the walls, Bass Orcutt couldn't stop eating and talking at the same time, half of his words losing their meaning by being strained through the beans, fat pork and hard bread.

Ross was hard put to keep looking at his plate. He didn't dare look at Consuelo.

"Yessir," said Bass proudly as he speared another slab of dripping pork and plopped it on his plate. "Times is changin' for good ol' Bass Orcutt. Not that I'm too old so's I can't keep up with you younger bucks." He leered suggestively at Consuelo and then at Ross. "Man can use plenty of strong sons on a place like this. They tell me the railroad may run a branch line through here. Soon as I can get me a real good water diviner I'll find water, sure as you're sitting there, amigo. With water, more cows, two or three sons and maybe a daughter or two to help Connie in the hacienda here, I'll be in the chips, I tell you."

Oh my God, thought Ross. There was no reason for the railroad to run a branch line down thataway, and water was a scarce item anywhere south of Deming, west of the Rio Grande and east of the Animas Valley. Further, if Tascosa had planted his seed in Consuelo, it would likely be the last of the Orcutts in that area, unless another wayfaring stranger with good looks and the qualities of a good stud came drifting through to stop at Bass Orcutt's 'hacienda'.

Bass waved his fork. "Yessir, Ross. You stick with me and soon's as I get things organized, you can ramrod for me. Take a few years and I can't give you no more than twenty a month and found, and mighty good found it is too!" He speared another slab of bread. He looked fondly at Connie. "Great cook! Good wife. Fine little woman! Begod, Ross, she'll make a fine mother too."

Ross shoved back his plate and felt for the makings. He looked politely at Consuelo whose face had taken on the wooden aspect of her part-Indian ancestry. She nodded, but there was murder in her liquid eyes. By God, she wasn't blaming Tascosa, the smooth sonofabitch! She was blaming Ross for letting Tascosa leave! Ross rolled a cigarette and lighted it at the smoking Rayo table lamp, direct from Montgomery Ward. He leaned back in his seat. Bass had been talking all the time. He had not noticed that Consuelo had left the room after placing the coffee pot on the table. Maybe she was hunting a *cuchillo* in the kitchen, sharp enough to cut Ross' heart out.

Bass looked up from his plate. "Beats the hell out'a me why Polk left," he said. "Fine fella. Good man with horses. Not the cowman you are, Ross, but you can't have everything. Where'd he go, you say?"

"I didn't say," said Ross cautiously. He filled his coffee cup. Connie's coffee was as strong as buffalo tea, as a rule. This night she had outdone herself. It would have been better than soda for cleaning an old rusted rifle barrel.

"Verde County likely," said Bass. He flourished his fork. "They wanted me to stay there and work for them, being a good gun, good man with stock and a fighter from whom laid the chunk, as the locals used to say. Tough enough to hunt bears with a switch, they used to say about me in them days. 'Course I was younger then. Not settled. Got a wife now and a hacienda, and no time for them goings-on."

Ross sipped his coffee. "What goings-on?" he said.

"All that trouble between that foreigner and old Hardy Newcomb. Newcomb ran that county like it was·his private preserve until that foreigner come along. Englishman name of Fitzgerald."

"More likely Irish," said Ross.

Bass shrugged. "Six of one and half a dozen of the other. Never liked him. Wore white collars into town and tweed suits. Begod, they say he et by candlelight when he had good mail-order lamps all over the casa! Took a bath every day too, they do say."

"Shocking," said Ross dryly. It was a good thing Bass Orcutt didn't require more water for washing himself at that. He rarely used it, except to water his rotten booze.

"Anyways," continued Bass, "all the trouble started because of property sold by Hardy Newcomb to that Englishman or whatever the hell he was. Newcomb is nobody's fool, I tell you! Sold that foreigner a lot of land, a sawmill and other odds and ends, then the foreigner finds out he bought the land and the mill and suchlike, but ol' Hardy had chivvied him out'a the *water rights!* Hawww!"

Ross emptied his coffee cup and looked toward the kitchen. It was dark. He had the uneasy feeling she was watching him from the shadows like a hunting cat. The hair crawled on the back of his neck.

Bass shoved back his plate, looked thoughtfully at the fly-specked ceiling and then belched deeply. "That's the ticket," he said in deep satisfaction. "Got room for coffee now."

"You were talking about Verde County," reminded Ross.

Bass filled his cup. He noisily sucked in half of the coffee. "Well, like I said, Fitzgerald was a dude, but he wasn't any coward. Some of them foreigners got guts too, they say, just like us Americans."

"Do tell?" said Ross in astonishment.

Bass nodded wisely. "Sure as you're sitting there! Fitzgerald went into court, but he was dealin' with a fox, I tell you. Besides, the judge was a cousin of Newcomb's, and the sheriff was his amigo in the war, fought all through it with Hardy, he did. Half that county seems related to ol' Hardy, or friendly to him anyways. Hardy always pays for a funeral when the Mex folks ain't got the money, and you know Verde County is about seventy-five percent Mex. You pay for a funeral for them and you got a friend for life, no matter what else you do. Some of them Mex gunfighters is hardcase, I tell you." He shook his head. "Some of them can fight durned near as good as Americans."

"I'd never have known *that*," said Ross wisely.

"Things quietened down for a time, after the governor put his foot down, but then the governor was changed, and the new man was an old amigo of Newcomb's."

"I might have guessed that," said Ross. He lighted a cigarette, glancing toward that dark kitchen. Supposing old Bass got wise? Maybe Consuelo would hang the blame on ol' Ross Starkey and let him take the punishment. It was a cinch she'd never tell on Tascosa. Maybe the damned fool thought Tascosa would come riding back like Lochinvar, or whoever the hell that waddie's name was in the poem.

"So Newcomb and Fitzgerald begins to go round and round again. Newcomb had most of the old Seven Rivers corrida riding with him by then and Fitzgerald had to re-cruit some gunslingers, so he lines up some of the old San Patricio bunch. You've heard of them?"

Ross rolled his eyes upward. "Some," he said. It was his old outfit. A good many of them had been shot to doll rags by the Seven Rivers boys years ago and Ross had lit a shuck for parts unknown, leaving no forwarding address.

"Anyways, it has been hell to pay and no pitch hot in

Verde County. Killings and beatings, and suchlike, and the governor sitting on his hands, waiting for the outcome. Hell, it's like a separate country down there, Ross! You got to choose sides. There ain't no walking the fence."

"And Tascosa went back into *that*?" said Ross, half to himself.

Bass slapped a hand on the table, jingling the tableware and tin plates. "I knew it was him all the time! Couldn't fool old Bass, I tell you. Funny thing, he didn't remember *me* in my gunfighting days in Verde County. But then I was never one to blow my horn, notch my guns, or nothing like that."

"Modesty is a virtue," said Ross.

"Exactly!"

Ross blew a smoke ring. "Who was Tascosa fighting for in them days?"

Bass reached for Ross' makings and deftly rolled a cigarette. "May surprise you. It wa'n't Newcomb at all."

Ross narrowed his eyes. "Fitzgerald?"

Bass nodded like a gooney bird. "Tascosa was just a kid when he first met Fitzgerald. Fitzgerald was a gentleman, like I told you. He treated his cowpokes like they was gentlemen too. Waste of time on most of them, but they say the Kid liked it. Maybe he wanted to *be* like Fitzgerald. *Quién sabe?*"

Ross nodded. It was the first bright thing Bass Orcutt had said in the weeks Ross had known him.

"Well, Fitzgerald can use the Kid, from what I heard in Columbus. Newcomb has got Fitzgerald up against the wall, I tell you. Folks say they figure Newcomb wants to drive that foreigner out'a business, keep him from getting the water he needs, chouse his men and rustle his cattle, then buy back the land he sold him at a quarter the price Fitzgerald paid for it. Nice profit too! Sharp as a Barlow knife, that Newcomb."

Ross yawned. "Time for the hotroll," he said. "What's on the docket for tomorrow?"

Bass looked up importantly. "Fence fixing," he said. "I brought back some rolls of wire and some staples. Got to get this hacienda area lookin' like something first, before we go ahead on the big plans, eh, Ross?"

"Sure thing, boss."

Bass seemed to swell a little. "Take care of that leg," he said. "Maybe Connie ought'a rub some liniment on it like she done on Tascosa's sore back some weeks ago. Good nurse she would'a made."

Ross shook his head. "I'll take a little walk to settle this good grub," he said.

Ross walked outside. He went into the shabby, sagging bunkhouse and gathered his gear. He stuffed it into a sack and then crawled out a back window. He went to the corral and got his horse. He saddled it, slung the warbag over its rump, then tethered in a draw beyond the barn. Ross walked back to the 'hacienda'.

Bass, happy as a clam at high tide, was helping Consuelo with the dishes. Ross got the saddlebags, making sure the rye bottle was all right, then took them to the bunkhouse. He changed into the good clothing Tascosa had given him. He sat for a while in the dusty darkness of the bunkhouse, nipping at the first bottle of rye, and smoking half a dozen cigarettes. When the lights had winked out in the casa, Ross slipped out the back window again. He limped to the horse and led it a quarter of a mile from the ranch buildings, then mounted and rode toward the dim northern end of the West Potrillos.

He looked back through the darkness. God help Consuelo if her firstborn was the spitting image of Tascosa. Maybe then Bass Orcutt would realize just exactly what kind of luck the Kid had brought him.

CHAPTER FIVE

Ross TURNED OVER in his sleep, then suddenly raised himself on one elbow. He tried to blink the sleep out of his eyes. The moon was almost gone and a mournful wind crept through the canyon rustling the trees and swaying the brush. The faint rush of the creek water came to him. The wind had shifted since dusk, bringing with it the faint suggestion of rain. Ross shivered. He pulled on his boots and clapped his hat on his head, then felt for his Winchester. He was too far north for Apache trouble, but even then the Mescaleros had been tagged and put on a reservation for some years.

Far down the canyon a horse whinnied shrilly, and the sound carried clearly to Ross. His own horse was picketed up a small box canyon behind him. An eye of fire showed in the ashes of his campfire, like a ruby on velvet. He kicked dirt over it, shoved his blanket and tarp under a bush, then padded down the slope until he found cover in a nest of rocks.

Deep shadows had formed along the west wall of the canyon, but the creek bed was still lighted by the dying rays of the moon.

Something moved up the canyon and then Ross saw a lone horseman, riding fast, rifle across his thighs, looking to right and to left, and then ahead again. He looked up the slope, almost directly at Ross, then away again.

A steer bawled. Hoofs thudded on the soft ground. A bunch of cows appeared through the swaying brush, running as fast as they could go, with a trio of horsemen driving them, one on either flank and one behind.

"Sticky loopers," said Ross. He sank a little lower. Rustling was good business in Verde County, or at least it had been.

The place was thick with tangled canyons, many of which led down to the lower country south, east and west, so a rustler could pick and choose his way to bedevil his pursuers.

They were moving fast. They thudded past Ross' position, not more than a hundred yards away, lashing at the flanks of the steers with their quirts, looking back from where they had come. In five minutes they were out of sight, leaving behind them the churned track, wide enough for a blind man to see, and the acrid odor of fresh droppings.

Ross felt the cold sweat break out on his forehead. "This ain't no place for Mrs. Starkey's second son," he said. He scuttled up the slope and hastily threw his gear together. Hot haste was in him. Hang first and ask questions afterwards was the current style of thought in Verde County.

He carried his gear to the horse, saddled it, threw his gear aboard and mounted the claybank. He slapped it on the rump with the butt of his Winchester and rode out of the box canyon, looking back in the direction from which the rustlers had come. Something was moving there in the darkness beyond the light of the moon. "Chihuahua," said Ross. He galloped the claybank, heading along the line of tracks. The ground was soft after a recent rain, and he had no desire to break his tracks away from those of the rustlers; not yet, anyways.

He crossed a wide patch of moonlight. A rifle flatted off and the slug whispered a foot past Ross' head. The rifleman had eyes like an Apache. Ross wrenched the claybank to one side and clattered over some loose rock, looking back over his shoulder. Something flashed and a fraction of a second later the rifle sounded off. The slug sang eerily from a rock.

Ross plunged into a wide draw. The claybank had hard going on the loose rock. Once he almost went down. Men yelled down in the canyon as Ross set the horse at a steep slope, riding like a monkey on the back of the animal.

A shot cracked out and Ross' hat was plucked from his head. Thank God it had had a high crown. He turned into a side canyon and let the claybank full out. The ground was rocky, but a good tracker could trail him in better light. He turned into an arm of the canyon, hoping to God it wasn't a box. There was no one behind him, close enough to see

him anyway. He plunged through a branch of the creek,
followed the far bank, then went back into the shallow
waters, driving the claybank full out, showering the water in
crystal sheets to each side.

A wide canyon opened to his right, still lighted by the
moon. He had no choice. He slammed down it, looking
back over his shoulder, the thudding hoofs echoing from
the high walls. He could be heard for half a mile. The
ground was hard. He knew the claybank couldn't last much
longer at this pace.

Ross slid from the saddle and led the claybank up a
slope and into the shelter of some pinnacles of rock. He
slogged on, his weak knee bothering the devil out of him,
but there was no time to take it easy. Not with those shooting fools coming after him, and begod, he didn't have any
real reason for being in that country other than being a
wayfaring stranger, and that was tantamount to looking
for a free hanging, if he was caught near a sticky looping
job such as he was sure he had just witnessed.

The moon was long gone when he stumbled out on a rude
wagon track that led down to broken ground through scrub
timber. The bittersweet odor of woodsmoke hung in the now
windless air. Far down the slope a yellow eye of light stood
out like the orb of a cat. Ross wiped the sweat from his
face. He sheathed the Winchester and then sat down on a
rock to rub and flex his bad knee. He looked back now and
then, but the darkness was quiet. He had come through an
unknown maze of rock and timber and by the grace of
God he had not gotten thoroughly lost in the back canyons.

A faint invisible finger of wind teased his damp hair. A
drop of rain struck his nose. Ross rolled a cigarette and
lighted it behind the shelter of the rock. He shielded the
quirly in a cupped hand as he mounted the claybank and
rode slowly down the track. By the time he reached the
more open ground he had to stop to put on his worn slicker.

He used the light as his temporary goal and saw that it
was coming from a small ranch house. Must be getting close
to dawn. The rain slanted down in a silvery veil. He had
the urge to keep going, all the way out of Verde County.
He wasn't sure in the first place why he had come there
after a couple of weeks of drifting after he had left Bass
Orcutt's 'hacienda'. He had started twice for Santa Fe to

see his elder brother, once getting as far north as old Fort Craig, but then he had let himself drift easterly, across the Jornado del Muerto to the Jicarillas. Lloyd would have to wait to spout his: "I *told* you so, Ross. Never would listen to me. Isn't respectable, or profitable to drift all the time." And so on and so on. . . .

Ross looked back over his shoulder at the dim mountains. "A man could get hung or shot foolin' around here, hoss," he said.

The rain was still slanting down when he saw the *placita* beyond the rushing creek. He knew the country to the east much better than this area. Years past there had been many such *placitas* stippling the flanks of the mountains, guarded by their crumbling *torreónes*, but during the war, when Unionists and Texas Confederates had been beating each other over the head from El Paso plumb up to Santa Fe, there had been no Regulars left to hold the Apaches in check and the Jicarillas and Mescaleros had ravaged that country until there was hardly a living white man, American or New Mexican, outside of outposts of the contending military forces, from the Rio Grande to the Pecos, and from Signal Peak to Cougar Mountain. Only after the war had some of the New Mexicans crept back to their ravaged little *placitas* to try and take up the old ways. They hadn't reckoned on the Americans who had flooded into that fine cattle country after the war, ex-rebel and Unionist alike.

Ross rode across the creaking bridge. The rising water was inches below the bridge flooring. The single, winding street of the *placita* was empty of life although it was already early afternoon. Woodsmoke hung pungently in the wet air and smoke hung low over the old adobes, while muddy water the color of chocolate poured from the roof spouts into the street. Most of the adobes had a thick thatch of natural growths on top of them, so old were they. There was a strong odor of decay about the place. At the end of the street the church sagged against the nearest house. The old *torreón*, built to repel Apaches in days long past, had completely collapsed, partially blocking the muddy street. A mangy dog, soaked to the hide, slunk into cover when he saw the hatless gringo ride into town.

Mist hung over the nearby mountain, hardly distinguish-
able from the drifting rain. It would be an early winter.

Ross dismounted stiffly. His guts tightened within him.
He felt for the makings and found them soaked. He pulled
out a bottle from the nearest saddlebag and found it almost
empty. He emptied it and tossed it atop the nearest roof,
wondering if the extra weight would collapse the rain-soaked
roof. He tethered the patient claybank under a dripping
ramada. The rich odor of chile beans drifted to him from
across the street. He squelched across the mud, avoiding
the deeper puddles, feeling the cold water leak into his
boots. A wide, low building had *Santo Tomas Cantina*
printed across the front of it, although sun and rain had
long ago erased most of the paint.

Ross opened the door and walked in. Half a dozen candles
guttered in front of makeshift tin reflectors, as the draft
from the door caught them. Ross sniffed the thick air. He
had found the right place.

A short, thickset man looked up from a table where he
was spooning food into his mouth. "Please to close the
door," he said in good English.

Ross nodded. "There is food?" he said in Spanish.

"You are welcome to some of mine, señor. There is too
much for one man."

"Gracias," said Ross.

"Por nada."

Ross was served, at the long zinc-topped bar, a thick-
walled bowl deep with beans and oily rich chile sauce, with
good bread to side it, and a bottle of beer for a wash.

The man studied Ross. "You have lost your hat?"

"Wind blew it into the crick," said Ross. He scraped his
spoon along the bottom of the bowl, chasing the last elusive
bean. "Can you reload this bowl?"

"A pleasure!"

Ross reached across the bar and plucked a sack of Dime
Durham from the rack. He rolled a quirly while the proprietor refilled the bowl. The man looked at him. "There is
a hat here," he said. "Left long ago by a man who wanted
credit against his hat. It is a good hat. To you, two dollars."

"Maybe he'll be back."

The proprietor placed the filled bowl in front of Ross,
withdrew his thick thumb from the hot chile and thrust it

into his mouth to lick it. "No," he said around his thumb. "He will *not* be back. There was a matter of some cows found in, how do you say it, his poss . . ."

"Possession?"

"*Sí!* That is it! They were not *his* cows."

"So he doesn't need his hat?"

The man smiled, extended both greasy hands, palms upward, and shrugged eloquently. "In a *casket*?" he said.

Ross shoved two damp dollars across the bar. "It's a deal."

"You are not superstitious?"

Ross shook his head.

The hat was a little small, but Ross figured he could wet it and loosen it, when he had time. It would likely be wet enough by the time he got out of those hills and headed for Santa Fe. He had had a bellyful of Verde County. He placed the hat on the back of his wet head and began to punish the beans again.

"You are passing through this country?" asked the cantina owner.

Ross nodded. He sipped the beer. He didn't want to waste too much time around this *placita*. A sort of unholy haste was building up in him; an uneasiness that would not leave until he was far north, heading up the Rio Grande Valley once again.

"This is not a good country for strangers."

Ross looked up. "I ain't a stranger," he said. "Just a travelin' man."

"Santo Tomas is a long way off of the regular roads."

Ross gnawed a piece of bread, watching the man with cold eyes. "I like the scenery," he said.

"I am not being nosey, as you Americans say, but there is much trouble in Verde County. A man must choose one side or the other."

"Which side is yours?"

Again the extended hands, palms upward, and the eloquent shoulder shrug. "I am not a fighting man. My cousin Orlando rides with the Newcomb corrida and my cousin Gaspar rides with the Fitzgerald corrida. My brother Pamfilo died some years ago in this very place because he rode with the Seven Riders corrida and was in here when the San Patricio vaqueros came into town looking for booze and women, as they said." He pointed to a bullet hole in the ceiling and another in the dingy wooden frame of the cracked, gold-flecked bar mirror. "Pamfilo was very brave. *Muy hombre!* But, there were too many of them. Pamfilo did not go alone."

Ross finished the meal and allowed himself a gentle belch. He rolled a second cigarette. "Give me half a dozen Dime Durham. You got any chewin'?"

"Rock Candy, Winesap or Henry Clay?"

"Winesap. Two plugs."

Ross stretched his stiffened muscles. He had a long ride ahead of him, taking it easy on the claybank until he got out of these damned hills that seemed to move in on you all the time. He stowed away the smoking and chewing tobacco and paid his tab. He turned on a heel and heard voices outside of the cantina, and the faint jingling of spurs.

"Business," said the proprietor. He smiled widely.

Ross felt his heart catch. Like the man had said: "This is not a good country for strangers."

"There is a back door," said the man.

Ross nodded. He started along the front of the bar when he heard the front door bang open behind him. It was too late. He stopped in mid-stride. "Give me another bottle of beer," he said. He blew a puff of smoke toward the back bar, glancing in the mirror as he did so, the smoke shielding his look. A big man stood framed in the doorway, rain running down his yellow slicker and dripping from his hat brim. He was looking directly at Ross. Ross lifted the beer bottle and took a good slug of it. He might need it before the day was out.

"Señor Cassidy!" said the cantina owner. "It has been a long time. You do not often come over to this side of the hills. Luz Avita has been wondering where you have been."

There was no answer from Cassidy. Ross could hear other men talking outside of the cantina. "Come on, Cassidy!" said one of them. "Least we can get a drink or two before we go on!"

"Maybe we won't have to go on," said Cassidy. He walked to the end of the bar and looked down at Ross' empty chile bowl. "You servin' meals here now, Fedro?"

The proprietor shook his head. "I shared the chile with this man. He was hungry and wet. It was the Christian thing to do."

"For a price," said Cassidy dryly.

Spurs jingled in the doorway and a tall man bent his head to get inside. Water poured from his turned-up hat brim. He grinned. "Hey, Fedro! Get a mop! I brung the water!"

Fedro laughed. "That Señor Slim, always with the jokes!"

"Rustle a bottle," said Slim. "Rye all right with you, Ben?"

A short, bench-legged cowpoke came in. He nodded, his hard eyes flicking back and forth about the low-ceilinged room. He centered his flat eyes on Ross. "Rye is OK with me," he said in an expressionless voice. He never took his eyes from Ross.

"Shut that goddamned door," said Cassidy over his shoulder.

Slim kicked it shut. A lump of wet adobe fell heavily from the damp, sagging ceiling and struck a table. Slim grinned. "We better get that likker in a hurry," he said.

Fedro placed bottle and glasses on the bar. "This place is old," he said. "My cousin Ignacio promised to fix the roof, but, as you can see, it is raining now."

Slim filled the glasses. "Sure, Fedro," he said soothingly. "And when it's dry, what's the use of fixing it. But then, winter always comes, don't it? When we want a drink here we'll have to dig down through the roof to find it. Well, it'll save you buyin' a coffin, Fedro, eh?"

Fedro quickly crossed himself. "Do not talk like that," he said. He picked up a battered pan and placed it under the place where the adobe had left a hole in the ceiling. Muddy water began to drip rapidly into the pan.

"You got inside plumbin' now," said Slim.

Ross studied his beer bottle as though he had never seen one before, but he knew without looking that all three men were studying him.

"That your hoss outside, mister?" said Cassidy at last.

"The claybank," said Ross.

"Looks tired, and muddy . . ."

Ross sipped at his beer. "He is," he admitted.

"Come a long way, eh?"

"Some," said Ross. His beer was getting flat.

"Fast too, eh?"

Ross looked at Cassidy. "No," he said.

"Which way did you come?"

Ross turned slowly. "Who are you?" he asked.

Cassidy looked at Slim. "He wants to know who I am," he said.

"Tell him," said Slim. He downed his shot.

Ben downed his shot and refilled his glass. His flat eyes never left Ross. "His hat don't seem to fit very well," he said in his expressionless voice.

Cassidy's blue eyes flicked toward the hat. "Put it on square, mister," he said.

"I don't wear it that way," said Ross.

"In the *rain*?" said Slim.

"It ain't wet," said Ben.

"Put it on square," repeated Cassidy.

Ross picked up the makings and began to fashion a cigarette.

"Go get the hat, Slim," said Cassidy.

Slim opened the door and walked outside.

Ross wet the cigarette paper and placed the cigarette in his mouth.

Slim walked in, carrying Ross' bullet-punctured hat, thoroughly soaked. He threw it on the bar in front of Cassidy.

"Once more," said Cassidy. "Put that hat on square!"

Ross snapped a match on his thumbnail and raised it to the cigarette tip. Cassidy took two steps forward and slapped the cigarette from Ross' lips. "You hear what I said?" he demanded.

Ross fanned out the match and looked squarely at Cassidy. "If you were alone," he said, "I'd knock your gawd-damned teeth out'a your big mouth."

Cassidy smiled. He reached over and pulled Ross' new hat down on his forehead. "It doesn't fit, boys," he said.

"Figures," said Ben. "Because it ain't his hat." He looked at Fedro. "Where's that hat that was left here by that sticky looper?"

Fedro paled. He swallowed. "It's gone," he said.

Ben nodded. "Figures. That's it, ain't it?" he jerked a thumb toward Ross.

Fedro looked at Ross, with misery in his eyes. "Yes," he blurted out.

"Take it off," said Cassidy.

Ross took off the hat and placed it on the bar. Cassidy

picked it up and turned over the dry sweatband. "What's your brand?" he said.

"Starkey. Ross Starkey."

Slim narrowed his eyes.

"The initials in this hat are J.C.N.," said Cassidy. He picked up Ross' bedraggled hat and looked inside. "R. S.," he said.

The cantina was very quiet except for the dripping of the muddy water into the pan.

"We found this hat in Boca Grande Canyon," said Cassidy. "Left by someone who cut off from a group of rustlers to lead our bunch astray. You denying this is your hat?"

Ross shook his head. They wouldn't have believed anything else anyway. "I don't know anything about any rustlers," he said. "I was camping along the crick back there. I saw the rustlers go by and figured I'd better hightail out'a there in case I might get picked up by mistake."

"Oh, there ain't no mistake," said Slim. He leaned on the bar. "Ross Starkey," he added. "I've heard of you. You used to ride with the San Patricio bunch some years past, eh?"

"I won't deny that," said Ross. "I've been in Mexico since then."

"In Mexico? Do tell!" said Cassidy. He looked at his two partners. "He was in Mexico, *compañeros*."

Ross wet his lips. He wanted a smoke, but if Cassidy slapped the quirly from his mouth he knew he'd tangle with the man and that would be a damned fool stunt.

"He doesn't seem to know who we are," said Slim.

"We ride for Hardy Newcomb," said Ben, like it was being a member of the Round Table or something.

Ross couldn't help it. "Congratulations," he said.

Cassidy leaned forward. "How long you been riding for that damned Irishman Fitzgerald?"

"I ain't," said Ross. "Never have been."

"Fitz has been hiring gunfighters, they say," said Slim. "You a gunfighter, Starkey?"

"He looks more like a mangy hound dog," said Ben.

Ross looked at Ben. "You don't talk much," he said. "Whyn't we keep it that way?" His six-gun was trapped beneath his slicker. He'd never have a chance of drawing, and if these hardcases rode for Hardy Newcomb, he had an evil feeling they'd all be faster than he was anyways.

Ben shoved back his glass. "You've had your fun, Cassidy," he said sourly. "Now let's get down to business."

"I want no trouble in here," protested Fedro.

"Go get the marshal," said Ross.

Slim laughed. "Marshal? Here? They can't even afford a watchdog."

"You goin' to talk or not, Starkey?" asked Cassidy.

"I don't know anything about rustlers," said Ross.

Cassidy reached over and ripped at the front of Ross' slicker. The buttons scattered over the bar. Cassidy plucked Ross' six-gun from its holster and placed it on the bar. "Come on, hombre," he said.

Ross walked toward the door. He might have a better chance in the open at that. Slim opened the door. Ben thrust out a foot and Cassidy shoved Ross. He was catapulted through the doorway into the thick mud. He lay belly-flat, listening to Slim laugh, and sheer hate poured through his soul.

CHAPTER SIX

ROSS SLOWLY RAISED a muddy hand and wiped the thickest of the mud from his face. He could feel the cold water penetrating his trousers. The odor of fresh manure filled his nostrils. He pushed himself up on his hands and saw that he had targeted in on a pile of fresh droppings from one of the three horses tethered to the hitching rail. He closed his hands on the thick mud.

"Get up," said Cassidy shortly.

Ross got up slowly. He turned and the mud was in startling contrast to the drawn whiteness of his face. For a clear moment he saw the grinning face of Slim, the cynical look on the face of Cassidy, the flat, expressionless look of the man named Ben, and it seemed as though time stood still for that fraction of it.

It was madness, but the hate in him had burned away all fear and restraint. He hurled a gob of the filthy mud into Slim's grinning face and another toward Ben. They leaped back, cursing and clawing at their bespattered faces. Cassidy had made his mistake in not covering Ross with a gun, for Ross plunged forward, stiff-legged, muddy fists already driving at the thin air before they made contact with Cassidy, and when they did, the big man was driven back against Ben, knocking him down in the reeking mud underfoot. Slim yelled explosively, dabbing at his blinded eyes, dancing around like an angry stork on his long legs.

Ross sank a smashing left into Cassidy's lean gut, just above the gunbelt buckle, and as Cassidy bent forward, a muddy fist rose to meet his chin, snapping back his head, while a looping left, with no style whatsoever, burned against his right ear, driving him sideways where he tripped over Ben and fell flat on his face in the mud.

Slim could just manage to see now. He clawed under his slicker, and thereby undid himself, for a right glanced from his lean jaw while a left stoppered his open mouth, and he felt teeth crack. He raised his right but it was too late to stop a slamming one-two in his belly. He smashed back against the cantina wall.

Ben struggled halfway to his feet and a hard bootheel caught him just below the throat, driving him back over Cassidy. Slim bounced from the wall and roared in, throwing rights and lefts at thin air as Ross waited for him, then stepped in between the long arms and butted the long man in the chest, driving him back once again.

Ben rolled over in the mud, coughing   gasping. A bootheel hit him on the back of the head and nearly knocked him senseless. Cassidy got to his feet and swung a wild left that caught Ross over the left eye, shaking him, and a right poked into his nose, stinging it and drawing forth a flood of blood.

Slim leaped forward, shoving Cassidy to one side in his mad haste to get at Ross. Ross met him with three soft punches, trying to get footing in the thick mud. The long leverage of the tall man gave him the power to hit Ross back over a horse trough. He rolled over to avoid Slim's stamping boots. He gripped the tall man by one leg and stood up, upending him into the flooded gutter.

Cassidy threw an arm about Ross' head from behind, working the muddy surface of his slicker sleeve into Ross' eyes, while hammering at his kidneys with a hard right fist. Ross went down on one knee and a bootheel, unseen to him, cracked alongside his jaw. He rolled over, almost blinded, blood pouring from his nose, trying to avoid the booting he knew he was going to get.

One boot landed on his back and another boot caught him in the side and then he was free of them. He tried to get up and fell heavily, but no more blows came.

"I could smell the blood and guts all the way at the end of the street," a familiar voice said. "Now supposin' you three gentlemen let the man get up and take you on one at a time. By God, I think he could do it!"

Ross wiped the mud from his eyes and looked up, the rain slanting against his bloody, battered face. "Hello, Kid," he said around a broken tooth and a mouth full of salty blood.

The Tascosa Kid sat a fine gray in the middle of the street, the rain slanting down on him, dripping from his hat brim and glistening from his slicker. It also glistened from the cocked Winchester he held across his left forearm, the unmoving muzzle covering the three Newcomb waddies. He looked at Ross in astonishment. Then he grinned. "I'll be dipped in sheep shit!" he said. "Begod, my old riding partner from El Corralitos! You haven't changed much. How's Consuelo?"

Ross got slowly to his feet. His breathing hurt his side. He blew the blood from his nose. "You ought'a know," he said. "You dirty bastard, I'll swear you left me there to face ol' Bass when he found out the truth."

"I wouldn't do a thing like that!" said Tascosa in mock astonishment. "What's the trouble here?"

Ross felt his sore jaw. "These three hombres said I was mixed up in a rustling in Boca Grande Canyon last night. I told them I wasn't. They didn't believe me. I don't know where they was aimin' to take me, but I didn't think it would be a healthy place for Mrs. Starkey's second son Ross."

"Don't get mixed up in this, Kid," said Cassidy.

Tascosa smiled thinly. "Only three against one? Whyn't you go back and get the rest of the corrida?"

"Newcomb won't like this, Kid," said Slim. He picked a loose tooth from his mouth. "That bastard hits like a mule."

Tascosa suddenly touched his gray with the spurs, dancing it to one side while he raised the rifle a little. "Watch it, Ben!" he snapped.

Ben slowly withdrew his hand from the muddy front of his slicker while his flat eyes never left Tascosa.

"You got no call to get mixed up in this, Kid," said Cassidy. "You ain't ridin' for Fitz anymore."

Tascosa smiled winningly. "I *ain't?*"

Cassidy and Slim paled beneath the mud and blood, but Ben stood there like a block of wood, his eyes still on Tascosa like a snake trying to hypnotize a chicken. Some snake and some chicken, thought Ross.

The rifle seemed to have taken on new meaning now. Slim glanced up and down the deserted street. Every Mexican in town knew what was going on by now, but they weren't coming out into that street, for fear it would turn into a bowling alley for wild bullets.

"Get on them horses and ride," said Tascosa pleasantly.

Cassidy looked at Ross. "We want him," he said.

Tascosa leaned on his saddlehorn. "Toss your gun into the mud," he suggested, "then you go try to take him, Cass. I'll sort'a officiate like, with the powers invested in me by the Winchester Repeating Arms Company."

Ben raised his head. "Get off that hoss," he said flatly. "You got a big mouth with that rifle in your hands. Get off that hoss and meet me in the middle of the street, Kid."

The challenge hung in the wet air and four men stood there waiting to see what the Kid would do.

Tascosa shook his head. "I've got a royal flush, Ben," he said. "Now you three git!"

Cassidy held up a hand. "Hardy Newcomb will want this man," he said.

"Is Hardy Newcomb the law in Verde County?" asked Tascosa.

"Fitz ain't," said Slim quietly.

Tascosa patted the wet stock of the Winchester. "Right now we got Winchester law," he said.

The three Newcomb men untethered and mounted their horses. They rode out into the middle of the street. Cassidy turned in his saddle. "You ridin' for Fitz again then, Kid?" he asked.

Tascosa nodded.

"That's all I want to know," said the big man.

Their horses' hoofs squelched in the pasty mud. The only one who looked back was Ben, first at Tascosa and then at Ross, and if Ross Starkey had ever felt the foul breath of death in a man's look, he saw it now.

Tascosa waited until the three men were out of sight. "Get inside," he said.

"They might come back," said Ross.

"No, they won't. The news is more important to Hardy Newcomb right now than a shooting is."

"Meaning you?"

"Meaning me." Tascosa dropped from the gray and led it into the *ramada* beside Ross' claybank. "Christ! You ridin' plowhorses now?"

"He got me out'a that mess in Boca Grande Canyon last night."

"He didn't get you out *far* enough," said Tascosa dryly.

Ross walked inside and leaned against the bar. Fedro's head appeared above the bar. *"Madre de Dios!"* he gasped.

"Glasses," said Tascosa. "Pronto!"

Ross sipped at the strong liquor. Weakness poured through him. "You timed it just right," he said. "Another minute would have been far too much for me."

"You were doing all right," said Tascosa. He downed his shot and refilled the glass.

Ross tilted his head to one side and studied him. "Just how long was you watchin', Kid?" he asked quietly.

Tascosa grinned. "I saw the opening act," he said.

"Gawddamn you! I could'a got booted to a pulp out there!"

"You didn't," said the Kid casually. "Wipe that horn of yourn, killer. You're gettin' blood in your drinkin' likker."

Ross shook his head. "Beats the hell out'a me why I come here at all," he said. He rolled a cigarette.

Tascosa snapped a match on his thumbnail and lighted the cigarette. He smiled. "Maybe you was lookin' for your old ridin' partner," he suggested.

"Fat chance," said Ross. He blew out a cloud of smoke.

Tascosa knew. He had an insight into such matters, but he was smart enough not to press the point. "I'm headin' back to the ranch," he said. "We can make it by nightfall if we leave now."

Ross refilled his glass and downed the liquor. His side hurt. His nose and mouth hurt. His eyes stung. His fists were lacerated. He was cold and wet, far from home and fully fed up.

Tascosa picked up Ross' pistol. "Jesus God," he said wonderingly. "This yours?"

Ross nodded. "It's the one you had me supplied with back at El Corralitos."

"What do you use it for? Cracking walnuts?"

"Heads," said Ross. "Now shut up, will you?"

"You can't carry a beat-up old cutter like this if you want to ride with me for Fitz."

"I ain't ridin' with nobody for nobody," said Ross sourly.

"You'd better come with me anyway. You'll be safe there. No rough boys to take away your toys."

Ross slid the bottle into his coat pocket. He sheathed the Colt and walked to the door.

"Serafina Padilla has been asking for you, Señor Kid," said Fedro.

Tascosa turned. "She's married now, ain't she?"

"That shouldn't stop you," growled Ross.

Fedro smiled. "Her husband is working along the Sacramento," he said.

Tascosa smiled. "Where does she live?"

"The last adobe south of town."

"*Gracias*," said Tascosa.

They mounted and rode out of town in the opposite direction from that taken by the three Newcomb riders.

Ross looked at Tascosa. "Who choused those cows last night?" he said.

Tascosa grinned. "Some of my boys."

"I didn't see you with them."

"I had other business."

Ross snapped his cigarette butt from his thumb and first finger and began to roll another. "Does Fitzgerald know about it?" he asked.

Tascosa shook his head. "He needs help. He was fightin' a losing war with Hardy Newcomb. You got to hit back hard, amigo. You got to hit back harder than they do!"

"So you're taking over Fitzgerald's war? By egging on Newcomb? That ain't too bright, Kid."

Tascosa looked at him. "He's the only man in my life ever gave me a real square deal and treated me right. He got me cleared of that murder charge that drove me out of this country. Fitz can't win *his* way. If I can get Newcomb riled enough to start a real shootin' war, then we can make up the odds. We can't win this way, like I said."

Ross lighted his cigarette and looked sideways at the Kid. "And *you* think the Tascosa Kid can make up the odds? Just like that?"

Tascosa smiled coldly. "You seen what I done back there, didn't you?"

Ross rolled his eyes upwards. "Oh, Jesus," he said. He looked at the Kid. "I can't figger it out. *You* fightin' on the losin' side of a range war."

Tascosa's hand tightened on his reins. " It won't be the

losing side much longer," he said. "I got the ball rollin' now. It's Newcomb's next move."

"He's made it already," said Ross dryly. "I damned near had to pay the bill for you eggin' on Newcomb."

Ross was cold and wet but an even colder feeling came over him as he thought of the implications of Tascosa's words and the hard-edged tone of his voice. He remembered something else too: the killing look on the face of the man named Ben.

"Fitz will hire you on my say-so," said Tascosa casually. "You'll likely find some of your old San Patricio bunch riding for Fitz."

"I finished ridin' with them years ago. When the Seven Rivers corrida got through with us there wasn't enough of us left for pallbearers. I left this county fanned by their bullets. Besides, those three coyotes back there know I used to ride with the San Patricio corrida. It was Slim that knew about it. Bass Orcutt told me that Hardy Newcomb was hiring Seven Rivers boys and Fitz was hiring San Patricio boys."

"You know all about the feud then. Ol' Bass gave you all the dirt, hey?"

Ross nodded. "I told you that you should'a listened to him instead of bracing up to his wife all the time. By Jesus, you should'a seen the look on her face when she found out you had lit a shuck.out'a there. Man, oh man! She was fit to kill, I tell you!"

Tascosa laughed. He slapped his thigh and laughed so hard the tears came into his eyes. Ross looked sideways at him, still surly as a bee-stung bear. "It ain't quite that funny," he snarled.

Tascosa stared at him, gray eyes swimming with tears. "It ain't?" he demanded.

Ross couldn't help it. He remembered the look on Consuelo's face and the twitching of her outraged little strumpet's rump as she had gone into the house, and then he began to laugh too as they rode along a tree-bordered road, which was hardly more than a cowtrail, with the rain slanting down in a silvery veil.

Ross took out the bottle and handed it to Tascosa. "Well," he admitted. "It's worth a drink." He rubbed his sore jaw. "Come to think of it, I never paid Fedro for this bottle."

Tascosa spewed out a spray of pure rye. He stared at Ross.

"You didn't? By godfrey! That's the first time in the history of Verde County anyone ever beat Fedro out'a a drink."

Ross grinned, his face aching. It was good to be riding leg to leg with the Kid.

Tascosa took another drink and wiped his mouth. "I'll get a job for you with Fitz."

"No," said Ross flatly.

"You got any *dinero?*"

Ross shook his head.

"Then you can work for him. You don't have to do any *fighting,* amigo. Fitz has a great spread. He's breeding the best damned blooded cattle in the Territory. He can use a good stockman."

"I ain't no gawddamned stockman," grunted Ross. "I'm a cowpuncher. A waddie. By godfrey, if I could cook, I'd get me a job as *cocinero* so I wouldn't have to get mixed up in no shooting scrapes. I got a bellyful, I tell you, ridin' with the San Patricio bunch, and then with Zaldivar, the 'Champion of Liberty.'"

Tascosa did not answer. He knew Ross better than Ross thought he did. Besides, he had seen Ross in action at The Eye of God and in the muddy street of Santo Tomas, taking on three of the toughest boots in Verde County, one man against three, and the hardheaded bastard hadn't known he was going to get licked, and maybe maimed or crippled for life back there. It was food for thought, and Tascosa had taken it on himself to champion Sean Fitzgerald. He'd need every fighting man he could get, for although Tascosa would not admit it to anyone but himself, he knew the odds were high against Fitzgerald, with a stacked deck to boot.

"Maureen can take care of that face of yours," said Tascosa.

"Maureen? Another one of your friendly fillies? That's a helluva name for a Mexican gal."

"She's no filly! She ain't no Mexican! She's Fitzgerald's sister!"

Ross looked curiously at the Kid. He saw the tight white lines radiating from the corners of the Kid's mouth. He whistled softly.

"What does that mean?" snapped the Kid.

Ross raised a hand. "Peace," he said. "I didn't know you was soft in the *cabeza* for her."

"Who says I am? How could you tell? You ain't never seen her!"

Ross smiled. He took out the comforting bottle and belted a good one. He wiped his mouth and offered the bottle to the Kid. The Kid shook his head. "I don't want to ride through this country with a belly full of tanglefoot," he said. "You didn't answer my question," he added.

Ross deliberately drove the cork into the bottle. He deliberately slid it into his coat pocket and patted it gently. "Stay nice and warm, friend," he said to the bottle.

"Well?" demanded the Kid.

Ross felt for the makings. "In all the years I've known you," he said quietly, "since we was snotty-nosed kids back on the Cimarron, I never knowed you to talk so nicely about a lady."

"I never knowed you until a couple of months ago! You gettin' drunk again?"

Ross rolled a cigarette. "Why not?" he asked. "I wish to hell now I'd never crossed the Rio Grande. The only way to look at this county is through the bottom of a whiskey glass, pretty as it is."

The rain slashed down. Tascosa withdrew into himself as he led the way through dripping underbrush, following almost indistinguishable trails, fording rushing streams, guiding his gray through seemingly impassable natural passages that cut through rugged outcroppings of the basic structure of the mountain flank. He was like a Mescalero Apache in these mountains, thought Ross. Ross had known this country well in the old days, but he was thoroughly lost now, for the peaks and landmarks were shrouded in drifting mist above the thin, silver veil of the rain.

There was something else too. Despite Tascosa's thorough confidence in himself and his fighting ability, and despite his defiantly hurling the gauntlet down in front of Hardy Newcomb's imperious nose, to egg the hardcase rancher into a shooting war, there was something else. A shadow was riding his wet back; the shadow of death speaking in the flat tone of a rifle from ambush.

CHAPTER SEVEN

THE RAIN had stopped and a cold-looking moon had slid out from behind drifting clouds, to shed a clear light down into the valley of the Rio Dulces. Across the wide, rushing river, shielded by swaying cottonwoods, blinked the yellow lights of a large house.

Tascosa turned in his saddle. "There it is," he said. "The 'Shamrock' spread. The best spread on this side of the mountains."

Ross nodded numbly. The cold and the long ride had taken a heavy toll of him and he realized now that he had never fully recovered from his sojourn down in Mexico. The battle in the street of Santo Tomas had not helped any. Even the booze had not helped much. He swayed a little in the saddle.

"You all right, amigo?" said Tascosa.

"I'll be all right. Begod, is there any heat left in this world?"

They clattered across the creaking bridge. The *rio* was rushing along just below the thick floor planking. Tascosa spat into the water. "This'll help turn that ol' sawmill wheel," he said.

Ross looked at him. "Bass Orcutt said Fitzgerald had bought a sawmill from Hardy Newcomb," he said. "But he said Newcomb had chivvied him out'a the water rights."

"He did," said Tascosa. "Dammed up the Little Bonita, and wouldn't let a shot glass full of water through, claiming he needed all the water for his cows. Hell! There's enough water on Newcomb's land to flood this whole damned valley."

"So, how did Fitzgerald get around the lack of water?"

Tascosa grinned. "He hired a real sawmill man. Fella by the name of Buck Ellwood, from Michigan, who knows more about lumbering than Paul Bunyan. Ellwood takes the sawmill machinery apart and has the whole thing hauled down to a fork of the Rio Dulces, gets it set up and is ready to do business. Ol' Hardy Newcomb don't know about it . . . yet."

"What happens when he does?"

Tascosa shrugged. "We can wait and see. Newcomb has a sawmill on the Burrito and used to have a monopoly on all the sawmilling around this county. That's why he sold the old mill to Fitz, then cut off the water for it. Made a nice profit, the bastard!"

"Supposin' he don't like the new location of the sawmill?"

"What can he do? He can't stop the Rio Dulces and its forks, because they run plumb through the center of the 'Shamrock' and even Hardy Newcomb couldn't hardly dam the Dulces."

Tascosa stood up in his stirrups and whistled sharply three times, paused, then whistled twice. He drew rein and waited. The wind brought a faint whistle from the darkness of a motte that lay between the *rio* and the ranch buildings. Twice, then three times. The moonlight glinted from something polished. A rifle barrel, thought Ross.

Tascosa rode up the slope road. He glanced toward the motte. "Everything quiet, Pardy?" he called out.

"So far, Kid," answered the unseen rifleman. "Fitz has been askin' for you. Where you been? Chasin' fillies down to Santo Tomas?" He laughed at his own joke.

Tascosa swung down and opened the Texas gate, waving Ross through. He closed the gate and then led the gray toward the long, low stables. Ross whistled softly. The place reminded him of the fine haciendas he had seen down in Mexico.

Tascosa looked back. "Ain't this the best?" he said. "Makes Hardy Newcomb's spread look cheap by comparison, I tell you. This is all practically new, Ross. Built around the old place that used to be here."

"No wonder Fitzgerald wants to stick it out," said Ross.

Tascosa gave him a hand down from the saddle. Ross staggered. Tascosa led the horses into the stables. Ross leaned against a tree. He heard footsteps squelching in the thin mud. "Is that you, Tascosa?" a cultured voice called out, in a soft, pleasing Irish accent.

"No," said Ross. "I come with him. He's in the stables."

"Who are you, sir?"

"Ross Starkey. I knew the Kid down in Mexico."

"I've heard him talk about you."

Ross grinned. "Nicelike, I hope."

The Irishman laughed. "You two must have had quite a time down there. I envy you."

"You didn't miss nothing, Mister Fitzgerald."

"You know me?"

"I guessed it was you."

The rancher came closer and the moonlight shone on his face. He was a good-looking man, with clear blue eyes and a neatly trimmed blonde mustache, but there was a tinge of sadness on his face. He lowered a rifle and grounded it. "You must excuse me for carrying this," he said.

"I understand, sir."

"Who you talking to?" demanded Tascosa from the stable.

"It's me, Kid," said Fitzgerald.

Tascosa came from the stable. He smiled with genuine pleasure. "This is my riding partner from Mexico," he said. "He's been hurt, Mister Fitzgerald."

"So?" Fitzgerald looked at Ross' swollen face. "Thrown by your horse?"

Ross shook his head.

"Thrown by three of Newcomb's boys," said Tascosa quietly. "He done a little throwin' himself. By godfrey, Mister Fitzgerald, you should'a seen Ross here taking on all three of them."

"Three of them?" said Fitzgerald.

"Art Cassidy, Slim Bellew and Ben Miller."

"My God," said the Irishman. "And he came out of it alive?"

Ross shoved back his hat and passed a tired hand across his battered face. "If it hadn't been for Tascosa here, I wouldn't be standing here now."

"Come into the house then!" said the rancher. "I've had some experience in medicine. Was a pre-medical student at Belfast, but never finished. Had some experience in Africa as well, and Maureen is a born nurse."

Ross limped toward the big casa. His leg was deviling him again. Tascosa looked at him. "They said he had been chousin' steers in Boca Grande Canyon last night," he said.

"Whose steers?" said Fitzgerald.

Ross looked back at him. "Newcomb's," he said. "I was camped in the canyon when the rustlers come through there. When they passed I knew they was bein' chased. I figured it was no place for a stranger. I lit out and the guys doing the chasing saw me. I just got away from them by the skin of my teeth. I made the mistake of stopping too soon in Santo Tomas. They caught up with me there."

"But you had nothing to do with it!" said the rancher.

Ross laughed dryly. "Correct," he said. "But they meant to hammer something out of me, lies or anything else I could think up. Good thing I didn't know at the time who choused those steers."

It was suddenly very quiet. Ross looked back over his shoulder into the set face of the Irishman. "Who was rustling those cattle, Mister Starkey?" said Fitzgerald.

Tascosa's look was deadly in the moonlight.

Ross covered his bobble. "I thought I recognized some of the boys I used to know in this country some years ago. Couldn't be sure, of course. I had to get out of there in a hurry, I tell you!"

Tascosa went ahead and opened a heavy door set deeply into a thick adobe wall. Soft lamplight flooded out onto the wet gravel of the path and a drift of heat caressed Ross like a welcoming hand. He stood aside to let the rancher pass.

"No," said Fitzgerald. "Please go in." He looked at Ross' face, clear in the lamplight. "*Good God,*" he added.

Ross pulled his soaked hat from his head. He was standing on thick carpeting with his muddy boots. He suddenly felt completely out of place in this great house.

"Let me show the way," said the rancher. He walked down the long hallway. He looked back over his shoulder. "The study will be best."

"Study?" said Ross, rather stupidly. He looked at Tascosa.

"Where one reads books and thinks," said Tascosa wisely. He grinned as Fitzgerald turned to open a door. "Stupid bastard like you wouldn't know what it was for."

"When did you learn how to read?" grunted Ross.

"I been studyin' the labels on horse liniment bottles," answered the Kid.

Ross limped into the room. He looked around in astonishment. Two of the walls were lined with bookshelves, floor to corbeled ceiling, so high that a ladder, running on a brass track, reached up to the upper rows of books. Firelight from a large beehive fireplace in the corner shone on the rich leather bindings of the books. The floors were covered with rugs which he recognized as being from the Chimayo country up north. He had never seen any as big as this. The furniture was almost massive, with deep, rich leather padding. A large table, thick enough to stop a .44/40 slug or maybe a stampede of cows, stood to one side, with a big Rochester lamp on it.

"I'll get water, liniment and bandages," said the rancher. He left the room.

"Classy, eh?" said the Kid. "You ever seen anything like this before?"

"Only in a high-class bawdy house," said Ross.

"How'd you ever get in one?"

"I had a letter of introduction," said Ross.

Tascosa leaned against a wall. "The whole casa is like this. I been in every room except Maureen's."

"What's been holdin' you back?" said Ross.

Tascosa did not answer. He was looking past Ross.

Ross turned slowly and his battered face turned red. A young woman was standing in the doorway looking at him, and he had no doubt about who she was. She looked much like her brother, except that her dark brown hair had a tinge of redness to it. She wore a dark, wine-colored dress that matched her hair, and stood out in contrast to her creamy skin.

Tascosa straightened up. "Miss Maureen," he said. "This is my riding partner from Mexico, Ross Starkey."

She smiled softly. "Pleased to meet you, Mister Starkey," she said in a voice that sent a thrill right into the deepest inner being of Ross Starkey. He was suddenly acutely aware of the rising odor of horse manure coming from his clothing, brought out by the heat of the room. He hadn't shaved for five or six days and hadn't combed his hair in two.

"My brother said you had been beaten by some men in Santo Tomas," she said.

"He was doin' a little beatin' himself, ma'am," said Tascosa.

"Help him off with his outer clothing, Tascosa," she said.

"All of it?" blurted the Kid.

She laughed softly. "Sometimes I think you're kidding me, Tascosa."

"Who? Me? Not *me*, ma'am!" said Tascosa.

Ross looked sideways at the Kid. Begod, he had never seen him like *this* before! He remembered then the sudden anger of the Kid when Ross had shot off his *boca* about Maureen back on the trail. No wonder.

Tascosa gave Ross a hand with the ripped, filthy slicker. He pawed clumsily at the wet coat and as he peeled it off the rye bottle fell from one pocket and a half-chewed plug of Winesap fell from the other. The bottle smashed on the polished floor, luckily halfway between two of the Chimayo rugs. The rich, fruity odor of the rye drifted up to add to the overpowering smell of manure and horses that hung about Ross like a shroud. The look that Ross gave the Kid made even him wince a little.

Sean Fitzgerald came into the room with a pan of water and a tray covered with medicines and bandages. "Off with the shirt," he said. He looked down at the smashed bottle. "First time I ever saw a partly full bottle around you, Tascosa."

"Sir!" said Tascosa. "You know I don't drink that much."

"It's mine, Mister Fitzgerald," said Ross. "A little protection against the cold, and Tascosa here."

Fitzgerald nodded. "I think I know what you mean."

Tascosa worked at Ross' shirt. He peeled it off, revealing Ross in all his glory in a dingy, yellowed, patched and torn undershirt. Tascosa discreetly moved beyond the big table.

Sean Fitzgerald unbuttoned the undershirt and dropped it about Ross' lean hips. He looked at the bruised side, reddish-purple from hipbone up beyond the lower ribs. "God in Heaven!" he said. "You must have ribs like steel." He led Ross to a chair. "Maureen, bathe his face. I'll have to put plaster on that side."

Oh my God, thought Ross. She'll have to stand next to me now. "The street was pretty mucky," he blurted out.

"I imagine the Newcomb boys don't smell any better," said Sean Fitzgerald.

Maureen began to bathe Ross' face, and drifting through his own rank odor came the faint touch of lilac perfume and the sweetness of young woman flesh. He did not dare look at Tascosa. She looked down at Ross. "The Newcomb boys?" she questioned. "Were you fighting with some of them?"

"Three of 'em, ma'am," answered Ross.

She smiled. "I'd like to see them," she said.

Tascosa laughed. "I thought he was going to take all three of them," he said.

She turned slowly. "Where were you when all this was going on?"

Tascosa opened and then closed his mouth.

Go on, you bastard, thought Ross grimly. Tell the lady!

Sean Fitzgerald walked to a sideboard. He looked at Ross. "Bourbon, wine or rye? Perhaps a touch of Scotch?"

"Rye is fine," said Ross. He winced as she touched a tender spot on his face, staring steadfastly at her bosom, just inches from his eyes, trying to keep his mind on what was going on.

Maureen finished the job and stepped back to look at him. "There," she said. "You look better now, Mister Starkey."

"Go get him some fresh clothing," said the rancher to Tascosa.

When Tascosa had gone, Maureen left the room with the basin and extra bandages. Fitzgerald placed a whiskey glass on the table beside Ross and filled it, placing a cigar box beside the glass. Ross selected a cigar and accepted a light from the rancher. He drew in the rich smoke and sighed in satisfaction. "Prime," he said.

Fitzgerald lighted a cigar and sat down opposite Ross. "Tell me about it," he suggested.

Ross blew out a puff of smoke. This was chancy ground.

Fitzgerald inspected his cigar. "You mentioned the fact that the rustlers could have been men you had known some years ago. Tascosa once said you had ridden with the San Patricio bunch. The remnants of that bunch now work for me. It's possible you might have seen some of them last night."

Ross sipped the rye. It was the best grade and proof he had ever tasted. This was living, sore side, battered phiz and all.

"Mister Starkey?" gently reminded Fitzgerald.

"Are you asking me, or telling me, sir?" said Ross.

A log snapped in the fireplace, sending a shower of sparks up the chimney.

"I'm asking you," said Fitzgerald quietly.

Ross emptied the glass and pulled his undershirt up about his body, thrusting his arms into the sleeves. He got up. "I thank you for your kindness," he said, just as quietly as Fitzgerald had spoken.

For a long moment they looked eye to eye, then Fitzgerald waved his cigar. "Sit down," he said. "I had no right to question you that way. Please forgive me."

"Why?" blurted Ross. "You ain't done nothing but be kind to me, a stranger in your house."

Fitzgerald waved a hand. "We've come upon hard times here. I suppose you know something about it?"

"I've heard some things," admitted Ross.

"What do you think?"

Ross inspected his cigar. He did not speak for a few minutes, and when he did, it was in a low voice of measured words. "A man's land is his to protect. As I understand it, Hardy Newcomb is chousin' you. Well, if it was my land and my living I'd fight him to the bitter end."

"You're a fighting man, Mister Starkey. I can see that. I have been a soldier, fighting in Africa, and I am not un-used to violence, but I did not come to this country to fight for my property, and perhaps my life. I came here because there is a future here."

"And yet you can't go on like this," said Ross. "You're damned if you do and damned if you don't!"

"You've phrased it very well," said the rancher. He got up and paced back and forth, his hands clasped behind him and a line of worry and tension drawn on his high forehead. "I didn't realize the power Mister Newcomb has in this county."

"He *runs* it, Mister Fitzgerald, and don't you ever forget it. I should'a known better than to come back here."

"You've had trouble with him before?"

Ross grinned wryly. "Well, there was some question about some of his cattle bein' missin' one time. The Seven Rivers corrida wasn't ridin' for him at the time, but he had some hardcases that was just as bad. Newcomb paid off the Seven Rivers boys and they ambushed the San Patricio corrida." He looked directly at the Irishman. "The 'Paches couldn't have done no better. I lost some of my best friends in that fracas. There was nowheres else for me to go but plumb out'a Verde County, I tell you, with the devil settin' on my coattails. 'Course it was never *proved* Newcomb had paid the Seven Rivers corrida to take care of us, but we had been gettin' along with them fairly well for a time, for our mutual benefit, like they say. It was that what done us in. We never suspected they'd turn on us."

"Dog eat dog, if you'll pardon the expression."

Ross waved a hand. "You're right. The thing was, we didn't have nothing to do with rustling Newcomb's cows, not that we was innocent of borrowing a few strays here and there from other spreads."

"I see. You're not working now?"

Ross shook his head.

"Would you like to work for me?"

Tascosa walked into the room with clothing draped over his arm just as the rancher spoke. He looked expectantly at Ross, and nodded his head a little.

"No," said Ross.

"May I ask why?" said Fitzgerald.

Ross stood up. "I'm tired of fighting; leastways *that* kind of fighting."

"Damned fool," said Tascosa under his breath.

Fitzgerald warmed his lean hands at the fire. "Get dressed," he said quietly.

Ross nodded to Tascosa and looked at the door.

"You gettin' modest in your advancing age, Ross?" said the Kid with a grin.

"Something you wouldn't know about," said Ross. He peeled off his wet, filthy clothing and then dressed in the new outfit the Kid had brought.

"Ross is a top stockman," said the Kid.

"I'm a cowpoke! A waddie! A wrangler! But I ain't no stockman! I told you that before!" rasped Ross at the Kid.

Fitzgerald turned. "Try us for a week or two, Starkey," he said. "All you have to do is work on the ranch."

"Sure," said the Kid. "Ol' Tascosa will do your fighting for you."

Ross relighted the cigar and blew out a puff of smoke. "You nor anybody else don't have to do my fightin' for me," he said quietly. "That is, when it's *my* fight."

"You make me sick!" snapped the Kid.

Ross fanned out the match. "You can say the same thing

for me, regarding you, Kid," he said. "Don't chouse me tonight. I ain't in the mood."

Fitzgerald smiled. "Get a good night's rest," he said. "I can have the Kid corralled for the night if you like, so that he doesn't bother you."

Ross shook his head. "Maybe the Kid is the only amigo I got. Not much choice, but he's all mine."

"Come and see me in the morning," said the rancher. "We can ride together over the ranch and see the possibilities. Perhaps then you'll change your mind."

"Perhaps," said Ross. He picked up the wet clothing and followed the Kid from the house.

The moon had slid behind the low-hanging clouds as they walked toward the bunkhouse.

"How do you like him?" said the Kid.

"He's all right," said Ross absentmindedly. He was thinking of someone by the name of Fitzgerald all right, but it was Maureen, not her brother. Ross felt as though he had left a piece of himself back in that big casa. He had left pieces of himself here and there in his life, and quite a lot of blood, when it was pooled, but this time it was something different. Something he didn't quite understand, for, you see, it had never really happened to him before, although many a time he had been sure it was the real thing. It was crazy. It was loco. It didn't make any sense. But he liked it.

"The best there is," said the Kid. He looked back at the house.

"She sure is," said Ross.

"I mean *him!*" snapped the Kid.

"Yeah . . . How bad is this thing really, Kid?"

The Kid looked directly at him. "Damned bad," he said quietly, "and it's goin' to get a lot worse before it gets better."

Somewhere in the soft darkness a dog howled at the sky.

CHAPTER EIGHT

Ross had roped and saddled a horse for himself after breakfast, eaten while the gray light of the dawn had given way to the brighter light of early morning. Sometime during the night Tascosa had left the bunkhouse with several of the men. Ross had not met any of them, for they had all been asleep when he and Tascosa had arrived at the bunkhouse. There had only been three men at the breakfast table, an elderly horse wrangler with a limp called Greener, a younger pimply-faced man named Marvel who did odd jobs about the ranch, and the man named Pardy who had been on guard all night. All three of them had been remarkably close-mouthed with Ross. It seemed part of the atmosphere of the rancho. Rancho de la Rio Dulces was the name of the place, but Ross had given to understand that the locals all called the place the "Shamrock" spread. He liked that better anyway. Spic names had never appealed to him as being fitting for an American ranch, and yet Fitzgerald was hardly different from being a spic, for he was a foreigner too.

Ross had had his last cup of coffee and cigarette alone. He felt stiff and sore from the previous day's events, but more than that he felt at odds-ends, as though he had no business being in the Rio Dulces country, and worse than that, in Verde County. Verde County had been like a suburb of hell for him in past years. It hadn't exactly welcomed him back, either.

The sun warmed his back as he led the horse from the corral. The horse whinnied softly. A horseman cantered from the rear of the cluster of ranch buildings. Ross stared wonderingly for a moment, shoving back his hat, and then he remembered where he was, and that he was a guest on the "Shamrock."

It was Sean Fitzgerald, riding a fine, clean-limbed bay. He rode an English saddle, wearing funny-looking pants that bunched at his thighs like bloomers, and then tapered down to fit his legs snugly. Above the funny-looking pants he had on a tweedy coat, with a soft yellow scarf, like a cavalry scarf at his throat. One thing he had done, he had gotten himself a decent hat anyways, thought Ross. A soft brown Stetson.

Ross touched the brim of his hat. "I took the liberty of taking a horse," he said.

"I expected you to," said the rancher.

"I wasn't sure whether or not you really wanted to go," said Ross.

"I usually mean what I say, Starkey," said the rancher.

Ross hesitated.

"Is there anything wrong?"

"Ain't you packin' a gun of some kind?" said Ross.

"To wear a gun is to look for trouble," said Fitzgerald quietly.

Ross shook his head. "Go back and get one then," he said. "You might never need it, but if you do need it, you might need it in one helluva hurry!"

Fitzgerald smiled. "I see you are well armed," he said.

"I'd rather go naked in this country than go without my guns," said Ross.

"I thought you said you weren't a fighting man."

"Let's call my guns my insurance." Ross swung up on the sorrel he had saddled. "If I had any damn sense at all, I'd just head this cayuse due north and keep going until I hit the Canadian."

They rode toward the river. Ross opened the Texas gate and closed it behind the horses. He looked toward the motte, now fresh and green in the growing sunlight. There was no one to be seen, but he had been too long along the border not to *feel* things, and he knew someone was within that motte, with half-cocked rifle, likely watching the both of them. The place was almost like an armed camp. Come to think of it, reasoned Ross, it *was*.

Sean Fitzgerald didn't talk much during the morning, but pride was in his blue eyes as he showed Ross over the spread. If it hadn't been for the threat of Hardy Newcomb and his ex-Seven Rivers corrida looming over the Shamrock, Ross couldn't have thought of a more ideal layout for a man in the cattle business. The Shamrock had everything— grazing, water, timber and shelter, coupled with a natural beauty a man couldn't cash in on, but which was an asset just the same.

Just before noon they rode out upon a saddle-backed ridge that overlooked the rolling country to the east, drifting down in undulating fashion toward a distant watercourse that sparkled in the sun between grassy banks. "We can water the horses there," said Ross as he rolled a cigarette.

"No," said Fitzgerald. He looked sideways at Ross. "That is the Little Bonita."

Ross lighted the cigarette. "So it's still good water," he said. Then something came to him. "I thought Hardy Newcomb had dammed the Little Bonita."

"Further down, closer to my land," said the rancher. "At the foot of this ridge my land ends. It follows the line of the ridge to that grove of trees there, where the Little Bonita bends west. The dam is in there. If you look closely you can see the sun reflecting from the water backed up behind the dam. It's a natural spot for a dam."

"Seem to me that Newcomb needs that water like he needs a hole in the head."

The rancher nodded. He took out a silver cigar case and selected a cigar. The sun flashed from the cigar case. Ross narrowed his eyes. Something had moved at the edge of the woods. A crow flew off to the east, cawing loudly.

"Get off that hoss!" said Ross sharply.

"Why?" said Fitzgerald.

Ross threw himself from the sorrel and his weight drove the lighter man from the saddle. Just as they hit the ground a rifle flatted off near the grove and a faint puff of smoke drifted downwind while the echo of the shot rebounded from the ridge and then died away.

"Roll down the slope!" said Ross. "Pronto!"

The rancher did as he was told. Ross took the reins of both horses, keeping them in between himself and the hidden rifleman. He led the horses down the reverse slope out of sight of the rifleman.

Fitzgerald got slowly to his feet and brushed himself off. "Ruined my cigar," he said quietly.

Ross picked up the cigar case. "That was good shooting," he said. "Even if he did miss."

The rancher shook his head. "He didn't miss. It was a warning. It wasn't meant for you."

"How do you know?"

"It has happened before," said Fitzgerald. He selected another cigar and lighted it.

"We weren't on Newcomb land," said Ross.

Fitzgerald blew out a puff of smoke. "No," he said, "but it's evidently part of his campaign to harass me. Chousin', as you call it. By either name it is a dirty business." He looked at Ross. "You seem to have a sixth sense. I would have never known anyone was planning to shoot at us. How did you know?"

Ross shrugged. "The wind was blowing east. The bushes moved west. That crow took off in a hurry."

Fitzgerald nodded. "Why can't I do things like that?"

Ross rolled another cigarette. "You wasn't born out here," he said. "Even when I was a kid we had trouble with Indian raiders. Jicarillas mostly. Then Texans would drift over the line and run off some of our stock. Had to chase them for miles sometimes, and they had a nasty little habit of raising the dust with the cows, whilst you was hot after them, then leaving a rifleman or two, like that one back there, to dust you up a bit. My cousin Gil was killed that way. Fifteen years old."

"I have a lot to learn," said the rancher.

Ross raised his head. "You got men working this side of the range?" he asked.

"Not that I know of."

"Someone is," said Ross.

"There you go again," said the rancher with a smile. "How do you know?"

Ross pulled his hat low over his eyes. "Look," he said quietly.

Five horsemen had topped a flat-topped hill a quarter of a mile away. They rode slowly down the slope and along the little fork of the creek that stemmed onto "Shamrock" land. They were evidently looking for something.

Ross blew a smoke ring. He had an uncomfortable feeling.

Boca Grande Canyon was just to the north. It was where he had camped the night before and where the rustled cattle had been driven as well.

"Those are not my men," said Fitzgerald.

Ross walked over to the sorrel and pulled his Winchester from its sheath.

"No," said the rancher. "I want no trouble."

"Maybe you want to die talking peace," said Ross. "Happens I don't." He looked at the horsemen. "I seem to remember two of those horses. They were ridden into Santo Tomas yesterday morning by two of the three Newcomb men that worked me over."

Fitzgerald studied the approaching men. "We don't have to worry," he said. "One of those men is Sheriff Hurley."

"Yeh," said Ross. "Dan Hurley. Him and Hardy Newcomb was in the war together. I've heard it said that Newcomb put Hurley into office. Very handy for both of them, I'd say."

Fitzgerald looked quickly at Ross. "That's dangerous talk," he said.

"All the more dangerous because it's true," said Ross. He ground out his cigarette and rolled another. He wished to God he had pulled leather out of there that morning instead of joyriding with this loco foreigner. He still didn't know what had kept him from leaving.

"Mister Fitzgerald!" called the sheriff as they reached the bottom of the slope. "A word with you!"

The lawman and the man who rode beside him came up the slope, while the other three riders dropped a little behind. Ross vaguely remembered Hurley. In Ross' time in Verde County Hurley had been a civilian employee of the army, in some capacity or other, going by his old title of Major Hurley. Rumor had had it in those days that Hurley had been suspect by the government for some time in the matter of perfectly good government property that had been condemned and sold at a cheap price by Hurley to contractors for the Mexican Army. It hadn't been long after that that Hurley had bought extensive property in Verde County, with the advice and cooperation of his old army pal, Hardy Newcomb.

Ross forgot about Hurley and the other three riders, as he looked at the man who rode solidly beside the lawman. There was no mistaking Hardy Newcomb. His hat was set straight on his block of a head. His big cigar was stuck at an angle from his wide mouth, jutting out from his powerful chin. His salt-and-pepper dragoon mustache had been trimmed straight across. Everything about Hardy Newcomb was straight across. Hat, eyebrows, mouth, shoulders and big hands. Everything, that is, except his conscience. It was said that the devil himself couldn't have straightened out Hardy Newcomb's conscience, or his tangled machinations in Verde County business and politics. He *ran* Verde County; he *was* Verde County.

Newcomb's frosty blue eyes held Fitzgerald's, although once they flicked appraisingly at Ross Starkey, and Ross Starkey, despite his calm expression, couldn't help but feel uneasy. There was a primeval power and aggressiveness about the man that could set almost anyone ill at ease.

"Gentlemen," said Fitzgerald with a smile.

Ross looked past Hurley into the bruised face of Art Cassidy and the empurpled face of Slim. He felt some satisfaction at the sight. Begod, he had put the Starkey brand on both of them, at least. Ben was missing, but Ross knew it wasn't because he wasn't able to ride or anything like that. Ross was more concerned about him than the other three. Few men would challenge Tascosa to meet them face to face in the street, with holstered six-guns quick to the ready hands.

"Ross Starkey," said Newcomb, as though he was mouthing a dirty word.

"Howdy," said Ross with a smile.

Newcomb ignored him. He looked at Hurley. "He was likely in on the deal," he said. "He ain't changed much since he left Verde County some years past. He's ridin' with Fitzgerald, as you can see."

"The gentleman is my guest," said Fitzgerald.

Newcomb grunted deep in his thick chest.

Hurley smiled a bland smile. "Twenty head of Mister Newcomb's cattle were driven off night before last," he said. "They were trailed to Boca Grande Canyon, Mister Fitzgerald."

"I know nothing about that," said Fitzgerald.

"One of your men was trailed into Santo Tomas yesterday morning," continued the law officer, just as though the rancher had not spoken. "Another of your men held a rifle on three of Mister Newcomb's men, allowing your man to beat Mister Newcomb's three men."

"I'll be damned," said Ross.

"Shut up," said Newcomb flatly.

Ross shut his mouth. There was no real issue as yet. Besides that, he wanted no part or parcel of Hardy Newcomb. The old bastard never forgot, or *forgave*.

"Have you seen those cattle?" asked the sheriff.

"I have not," said Fitzgerald.

Hurley looked at Ross. "Have you?"

Ross nodded.

"Where are they?"

"Quién sabe?" said Ross. "I was camped in Boca Grande. I heard the steers being driven up the crick. I got to hell out'a there, I tell you!"

"Why?" said Hurley.

"Why? Hellsfire! If them Newcomb riders had caught me they'da strung me up for sure."

"They tried to stop you."

Ross grinned. "Yeh, with .44/40 slugs."

"You deny that you work for Mister Fitzgerald?"

"That's right."

"He's lying," said Newcomb flatly. He worked the unlit cigar over to the far side of his mouth.

"He does not work for me," said Fitzgerald flatly. "I do not know whose men those were who rustled your cattle, Mister Newcomb, or if they were anyone's men at all. I don't know where those cattle are."

"He's lying too," said Newcomb.

"Sir!" said Fitzgerald. His face whitened. "I give you my word!"

Newcomb took the cigar from his mouth and spat at the rancher's feet. "That's about the value of your word, you damned foreigner!"

Fitzgerald's face went white beneath the tan. His hands opened and closed but he managed to gain control of himself.

Newcomb shifted in his saddle. "Take Starkey along, Dan," he said, almost as though he was issuing an order.

Hurley smiled, a little unctuously. "Come on then, Mister Starkey."

"Where to?" said Ross.

"Just for a little questioning. No need to be alarmed."

"Where?" insisted Ross.

Newcomb fixed Ross with his basilisk stare, and Ross found it difficult to look into those icy, almost inhuman blue eyes. He could almost see the layer of hard ice beneath the surface. "You goin' to argue with the sheriff?" said Newcomb. It wasn't really a question, as he put it.

"I'll take you into Las Piedras," said the sheriff.

Ross looked past the officer, into the impassive faces of the three Newcomb riders. He knew his chances of getting safely to Las Piedras were pretty poor. Las Piedras was Newcomb country; in fact, the very heart of his "domain". He owned half of the town and the other half of the town likely owed him money, or worked for him, anyway.

"Are you coming?" said Hurley.

"You *askin'* him?" said Newcomb. He touched his horse with his heels and moved it a little closer to Ross.

"Have you a warrant for his arrest?" said Fitzgerald.

"Listen to *him*," said Newcomb.

"No," said Hurley. He seemed to be getting a little nervous. "I'm taking him in under suspicion."

"I'll vouch for him, Sheriff Hurley," said the rancher. "When do you want him in town?"

"Now!" said Newcomb. His three riders had moved forward, as he had done, as though drawn by invisible wires, or an unspoken command.

"Get on that hoss, Starkey," said Newcomb flatly.

Ross wet his dry lips. There was no way out of this one. He had grounded the rifle beside him but he did not dare raise it. He'd have a belly full of slugs before he got off one clean shot.

Hurley looked at Newcomb. "I'm inclined to take Mister Fitzgerald's word," he suggested.

"You'd take crap from him," said the big rancher.

Hurley flushed. "Now, Hardy!"

"Now, Dan!" mimicked the rancher.

Hurley looked uncertainly at Ross.

"You got your orders, Hurley," said Ross.

The wind shifted a little. It blew the horses' tails and manes and fluttered loose clothing. It brought something else too. The soft sound of hoofs thudding on the ground southwest of where the stand-off was between Ross and the law.

Cassidy shifted in his saddle. " 'Shamrock' riders, Mister Newcomb," he said.

Newcomb looked toward the newcomers. There was no expression on his face. "It's that babyfaced killer," he said.

"He's got eight men with him," said Slim.

"I can count!" snapped Newcomb.

Hurley rubbed his smooth, rounded jaw. He looked at Fitzgerald. "Bring him into Las Piedras tomorrow," he said.

Newcomb spat again. He shifted his cigar to the other side of his mouth. He looked at Ross and then at Fitzgerald. "You heard the man," he said. He turned his horse, then looked at Ross again. "If Dan lets you go, Starkey, you just keep *on* goin'. You hear?"

Ross nodded. He knew well enough what Newcomb meant.

The Newcomb party rode toward the ridge. They stopped at the top of it and looked back as Tascosa and the "Shamrock" riders loped up to Fitzgerald and Ross, rifles across their thighs. Tascosa waved his hat at the Newcomb party. "The ranch line is due west!" he called out. He grinned.

When Ross looked again the Newcomb party was gone, but they had left something behind them; a cold, hostile feeling that had settled about Ross and the "Shamrock" men like a chilling, miasmic mist from some long-forgotten swamp.

Ross felt for the makings. "You reached here just in time, Kid," he said.

"Lucky for you," one of the riders said. He grinned. "Hello, Starkey!"

Ross nodded. "Hello, Mac," he said. "You been all the time in Verde County since I last saw you?"

Mac McArthur grinned again. "Well, not always. Got to admit the Seven Rivers boys dusted us a little too much some years past."

"Yeh," said Ross dryly. "You can say that again."

"*Hola*, Ross," said a pleasant-faced Mexican.

Ross narrowed his eyes. "Do I know you?"

"I think so. I am Francisco Ochoa."

Ross lighted his cigarette. "Ochoa? I knew a Diego Ochoa in the old days." His voice trailed off. He remembered all too well what had happened to Diego Ochoa.

"*Mi hermano*," said Francisco with a proud smile.

Ross nodded. "You were just a kid then, Francisco, and now you are a man. *Muy hombre!*"

"My brother always spoke well of you. Now it is I who rides with Ross Starkey, *and* the Tascosa Kid!" His white teeth shone beneath his thin mustache as he looked proudly at Tascosa.

Ross blew out a puff of smoke to hide the feeling reflected on his face. Diego Ochoa had had his back broken by a slug in the ambush so many years ago. Writhing and twisting on the dusty ground, calling for his God and his mother until a softnosed slug had smashed into his screaming mouth.

"My brother died well," said the young Ochoa.

"Muy hombre," agreed Ross. Perhaps you will die well too, little brother, he thought.

Tascosa swung down from his horse. "Joe Bacon spotted you two, Mister Fitzgerald," he said. "Lucky we was workin' along the fork at the time."

Fitzgerald nodded. There was a deeply thoughtful look on his face. "I don't like this," he said, almost to himself.

"You got to fight fire with fire," said the Kid.

Fitzgerald looked angrily at him. "Do I? This is no way to live! Armed men patrolling either side of the boundary. Waiting for a chance to shoot and kill! Why, Ross and me were shot at from that grove near the dam pond not more than an hour ago."

"You were?" said the Kid thoughtfully. He looked at Mac McArthur. McArthur turned his horse and rode along the bottom of the ridge.

"I want no trouble," said Fitzgerald.

"There won't be any, sir," said the Kid cheerfully.

Fitzgerald mounted. Ross slid the Winchester into its saddle scabbard and mounted the sorrel.

"Was you aimin' to do some rabbit shooting?" said the Kid.

"Skunk," said Ross dryly. He looked at Tascosa. The Kid knew well enough what he meant.

Ross and the rancher rode down the slope back toward the distant ranch buildings on the far side of the Rio Dulces. When they reached the first line of timber, Ross looked back. Seven men were riding north. The Tascosa Kid was missing. Ross had a damned good idea where he had gone.

CHAPTER NINE

Dusk had filled the valley of the Rio Dulces and a cold wind whispered through the trees and brush, moaning softly about the ranch buildings and whining from the tops of the broken hills behind the river valley. It was very quiet about the ranch as Ross saddled his claybank. The bunkhouse was empty. The only sound of man about the area was the rattling of pots and pans in the cookhouse. Ross closed his saddlebags and led the claybank from the stable. He looked up at the night sky. It would rain before morning if the wind kept coming from the northeast. He looked over toward the big casa. He wanted to say goodbye to Sean Fitzgerald and Maureen as well, although he had not seen her since the time she had helped minister to his wounds. He had not forgotten that. The memory was acute. More than ever he now realized that there was a wide gap in his life, and it was widening day by day. Maybe there was something after all in a man settling down with a wife, raising a few kids. How long could he be a lobo, riding the owl-hoot trails, with no roof over his head. "The son of man has no home," he said as he led the claybank toward the gate.

A shadowy figure moved in amongst the trees that were between Ross and the big casa. Ross dropped his hand to his Colt.

"Is that you, Starkey?" said Sean Fitzgerald.

"Yes sir, Mister Fitzgerald," said Ross. Damn it! He hadn't wanted to face the rancher, leaving like this in the dark of the moon.

"Where are you going?"

Ross took his hand from his Colt as the rancher walked toward him. The wind carried the faint sound of voices from the river bottoms.

"Starkey?" said the rancher.

Ross wet his lips. Maybe Fitzgerald had been waiting for him.

"You're planning to leave, permanently. Is that it, Starkey?"

"Yes," admitted Ross.

"Have you forgotten that I agreed to bring you to Las Piedras tomorrow?"

"It was your idea, not mine."

"I more or less gave my word on it."

Hoofs thudded on the road beyond the fence line.

"Then you can forget about it," said Ross.

"I can't do that," the rancher said quietly.

"You don't know who you're dealing with!"

"I think I know you."

"Listen," said Ross impatiently. "They won't bother you. They know about me from the past. They won't ever forget that fracas in Santo Tomas. They only got one way of taking care of such debts and it ain't by being peaceable-like."

"I agreed to take you there," said Fitzgerald.

The horsemen were at the gate. It creaked open.

Ross swung up on the claybank. "Leave that gate open!" he called out.

"That you, Ross?" called Tascosa.

"It is."

"Where are you going?"

Ross touched the claybank with his spurs. He looked at the rancher. "I'm sorry," he said, "but it's got to be this way. Say goodbye to Miss Maureen for me, and thank her for me."

"I thought better of you than this," said Fitzgerald.

Ross had no answer. He rode toward Tascosa. The Kid leaned forward in his saddle. "What's the trouble, Ross?" he said.

"There isn't any. I'm just leaving."

The Kid looked at Fitzgerald. "What's goin' on here?" he asked.

Fitzgerald shrugged. "Ask your friend Mister Starkey," he said.

"Well, Ross?" said the Kid.

Ross felt his temper rise a little. "I'm headin' out," he said. "Mister Fitzgerald took it on himself to promise to deliver me into Sheriff Hurley's hands tomorrow in Las Piedras."

"That don't make sense," said the Kid.

The rancher shook his head. "They would have taken him before you got there this afternoon," he said. "It was the only way I could get him out of their hands."

"And you still aim to take him there tomorrow?"

"I gave my word on it."

"His word," said Ross. "Not mine."

"Your word ain't worth crap," said the Kid.

Ross looked closely at the Kid. Tascosa's face was set and the danger lines showed at the corners of his mouth.

The Kid looked back at his two companions. "Go on to the bunkhouse," he said.

They rode wordlessly away, looking back over their shoulders. One of them was the man McArthur Ross had known in the old days on the San Patricio.

"Get off that hoss," said the Kid to Ross.

"I ain't taking orders from you," said Ross.

Tascosa smiled, but there was no mirth in his cold eyes. "You *ain't?* Mister Fitzgerald said he was goin' to take you into Las Piedras tomorrow. *You* are going to *go* with him."

It was very quiet now, except for the soft whispering of the wind along the river bottoms and the faint creaking of swaying branches.

"Get out of the way, Kid," said Ross.

"Let him go, Tascosa," said Fitzgerald. "I don't want any more trouble."

"You said you was goin' to take him into Las Piedras. That's good enough for me. He's going," said the Kid flatly.

A cold anger filled Ross. He wanted no part or parcel of the Kid, and he didn't want to back down in front of him.

"*Get off that hoss,*" said the Kid.

Ross wet his dry lips. "I ain't taking orders from you, nor anybody else around here," he said. "I don't work here."

"Listen," said the Kid thinly. "Mister Fitzgerald give his word. That's something you wouldn't know about, and me neither. He's a gentleman. Them things mean a lot to him."

"They don't mean nothing to me," said Ross. "All I know is that Hardy Newcomb will take any chance he can to get at me. Nobody crosses him and gets away with it. He thinks I had something to do with stealin' those cows. He believes it.

Christ hisself couldn't bear witness for me that I didn't do it and you know it. You tryin' to get me killed? Maybe Mister Fitzgerald will be, too, for all we know."

The Kid shook his head. "Nobody is goin' to get killed. I'll make sure of that."

"I want no armed guards," said the rancher. "You know better than that. A mob of armed men riding into Las Piedras will be the gauntlet flung down; the open challenge. No, Tascosa, I won't have it!"

The Kid smiled. "It'll be all right," he said. "I'll ride along with you two."

"Gee," said Ross, "that'll make it just jimdandy!"

The Kid nodded. "Take that hoss back," he said pleasantly.

It was no use. Ross had been bluffed out. He knew the Kid wouldn't hesitate to draw and shoot. Fitzgerald was like a chieftain to him, or perhaps a god. Nothing else mattered. Ross was nothing, if Fitzgerald's desires were to be frustrated by him. He carried no guns. With the Kid around he didn't have to. It wouldn't always be that way.

Ross dismounted and led the claybank toward the corral. The Kid said something in a low voice to Fitzgerald and then rode after Ross. "What's for grub tonight?" he said.

Ross did not answer. He stopped at the corral and opened the gate, with the Kid sitting his horse, one forearm resting across his saddlehorn. "You ain't talkin' to me, hey?" said the Kid.

"You got the general idea," said Ross.

"It'll be all right tomorrow with me there."

"Sure, sure," said Ross. "Little Jesus walks the streets of Las Piedras."

"That ain't funny!"

Ross unsaddled the claybank and slapped him on the rump. He slung the saddle over the top corral rail and looked at the Kid. "No," he said quietly. "It *ain't* funny. It ain't funny at all. I ain't forgettin' this, Kid." He walked out of the corral and walked toward the bunkhouse, feeling for the makings.

"Don't get any ideas of slippin' out of here tonight," said the Kid.

This time it was hate that poured through Ross' soul, but he was too good a poker player to make his bid now. The Kid had all the aces.

Ross walked into the bunkhouse. McArthur lay on his bunk, lean hands clasped behind his head, his amused eyes on Ross. The other man was seated at the table, cleaning his revolver. "You're Starkey, hey?" he said. He looked at Ross with his one eye. The other was a glassie, and the color of it didn't quite match the other. "I'm Joe Bacon. I've heard of you from the Kid."

"Howdy," said Ross. He shoved back his hat and began to roll a cigarette.

"You workin' for Fitz now?" said the one-eyed man.

"No."

"Then how come you take orders from the Kid?"

Ross ran the cigarette paper across his lip and twirled the paper cylinder. He lighted it from the table lamp.

"I ast you a question," said Bacon.

"I heard you," said Ross.

McArthur looked at the ceiling. "The Kid likes to give orders," he said.

"What does that mean?" said Bacon.

McArthur looked at Ross. "Somebody's got to give them around here. Fitz is a nice hombre, but man, he don't know from nothing about runnin' a spread like this. The Kid is practically boss here now."

"It's that filly up to the casa," said Joe Bacon. He lovingly wiped the cylinder and barrel of his Colt and then began to feed shiny cartridges into it.

"Crap," said McArthur. "It's Fitz he works for, not her."

Joe closed the loading gate of the Colt. "Maybe he's workin' for the whole spread, *and* her. The Kid don't worry about such matters as loyalty and suchlike."

"Like you," said the lean man in the bunk. He grinned.

Joe looked at him and the glass eye seemed to move of its own accord. "I ride for whoever pays me the most," he said. "Fitz pays me better than Newcomb did and he has better grub."

"You got a simple philosophy," said Mac.

"What the hell is that?" asked Bacon.

"You wouldn't know," said Mac.

The glass eye swiveled. Joe looked in Ross' general direction. "You never answered me about the Kid," he said.

"Lay off, Joe," said McArthur.

"I want to know."

Ross sat down on a chair and rested his arms on the back of it. He blew a smoke ring and moodily watched it waver in the heat of the lamp, rise, and then drift toward a partly open window.

"You hear me?" said Joe.

Ross looked at him. It was disconcerting as hell, trying to look into the one good eye with that glassie wobbling around. "It ain't none of your damned business," he said flatly.

Joe's face went white beneath the tan. His hand tightened about the butt of his Colt. "Ain't nobody can talk to me like that!" he snarled.

"Except the Kid," said Mac. He grinned again.

Ross knew there was something loose in Joe Bacon besides the glass eye. "Sit down," he said quietly. "I don't want any trouble and I don't feel like answering questions."

Joe walked toward him, the polished Colt swinging back and forth, reflecting the lamplight. He stopped five feet from Ross. "I'm the big rooster in this corrida," he said. "You'd better know that, Starkey."

For the first time Ross felt a twinge of fear. The man wasn't quite right, or he wouldn't have pressed his senseless question.

Joe raised the Colt and the smell of the fresh oil drifted to Ross. The hammer snicked back to half cock. "I ast a question," he said softly.

The door opened and the Kid walked in. He flicked his eyes about the smoky room. "Mac, go out and relieve Francisco at the gate."

The lean puncher dropped his long legs to the floor, but he didn't move from the bunk, watching the play between Ross and Joe.

The Kid looked at Joe. "Put up that cutter," he said.

Joe swiveled his one good eye. "He won't answer a question of mine," he said.

The Kid smiled. "My amigo is a stubborn man, Joe."

The gun muzzle centered on the Kid's gunbelt buckle. "All I wanted was an answer," said Joe.

The Kid studied the older man. "Put that damned gun where it belongs," he said. He didn't have a chance of drawing if Joe's unstable mind let slip its sear.

For a long moment Joe stood there. His glass eye moved.

"I *said*: *Put that damned gun where it belongs*," said the Kid.

Joe's one good eye looked away. The glassie did a little dance of its own. The Colt was slid into its shaped holster. "All I did was ast a question," he said defensively. He turned and walked to his bunk.

"What's holdin' you back?" said the Kid to McArthur. "I told you to get out to that gate!"

The tall man flushed. He picked up his rifle and walked out of the bunkhouse.

Ross dropped his cigarette into the butts can and began to roll another. Whatever else the Kid had, or didn't have, there was one thing sure; he could give orders to older men, tough hardcases that maybe even Hardy Newcomb might have had a little trouble handling, and Hardy Newcomb was at least thirty years older than the Tascosa Kid.

The Kid looked at Ross. "Time for grub," he said.

"I ain't hungry."

Joe Bacon put on his hat and left the bunkhouse.

"Nice fella," said Ross as he lighted up.

"He's a fightin' man," said the Kid. "Ain't afraid of nothing."

"Except you," said Ross, looking sideways up at the Kid. "He ain't that loco."

The Kid took the makings from Ross' pocket and began to roll a quirly. "There's a bottle in my warbag," he said.

"I ain't thirsty."

"That's a switch." The Kid lighted the cigarette and blew a puff of smoke toward the lamp. "You're still waspy, hey?"

"I got a low boilin' point," said Ross.

The Kid shrugged. "I'll get some grub," he said. "If Francisco comes in tell him to come over and get some grub. I got something to tell him."

"Is that an invitation or an order?"

The Kid took the cigarette from his mouth. "You know," he said conversationally, "you're beginning to annoy me."

Ross slowly stood up. "You been annoyin' me for a long time," he said. "There's ways we can settle it."

The Kid smiled. "Not with *guns*, hombre."

"I can't outdraw you, Kid. I wasn't thinkin' of a shooting scrape."

The Kid shrugged again. "Maybe you're thinkin' of going

out behind the stables, bare knuckles to a finish, hey?"

Ross unbuckled his gunbelt and hung it over the chair.

Tascosa dropped his cigarette into the butts can. "You know," he said quietly. "You got an idea you're the big augur with them fists of yours. Somebody just ought'a take that idea out of you, maybe through the hide."

"Like you?"

The Kid smiled. "You were wide open most of the time in that street picnic in Santo Tomas."

Ross walked toward the door. "Come on," he said. "Put your fists where that big mouth is."

The Kid did not move.

Ross turned. "You yella without that gun?" he said. He knew the Kid would never take that one.

The Kid's face went white. He opened and closed his mouth. For a fraction of a moment his lean hands lingered just over his gunbelt buckle and then he moved them to his sides. "I got plans," he said. "I can't afford to get tangled in a fight with a damned hotheaded fool like you."

"Hear, hear," said Ross sarcastically.

"Grub pile!" yelled Baldy the cook from the cookhouse.

The Kid began to fashion a smoke. He placed it between his lips and lighted it. He walked to the door, right past Ross. He looked squarely into Ross' eyes and Ross knew it wasn't fear that had held the Kid back from a bare-knuckled jamboree atop the old manure behind the stables.

Ross put on his gunbelt after the Kid had left. He was still sitting at the table when Francisco Ochoa walked in. "*Hola*, amigo," said the kid.

Ross nodded. "Little Jesus wants to see you over at the *dinin'* hall," he said.

Ochoa narrowed his eyes. "Little Jesus?"

"The Kid."

Francisco leaned against the wall. "You do not like him?"

"I can live without him," said Ross dryly.

"He is one of the great ones," said Ochoa. "Fast like the striking *uiboras cascabeles* with the six-gun."

Ross spat. "A rattlesnake has got more morals," he said.

"You had better not let him hear you say that!" said Ochoa angrily.

"Who? The rattlesnake? I'd be ashamed to say it to one of them."

Ochoa felt for the makings. He began to roll a cigarette. "He always talked highly of you," he observed.

"Because he could use me."

"Is it not true that without him you would have died in Mexico, up against a wall, or perhaps in the desert north of the prison from which he helped you to escape? Did he not save you from the Apaches? Did he not save you from those men in the street of Santo Tomas? Are you not grateful?"

Ross shook his head. "He didn't miss much, did he?"

"He is the greatest of them all," said Ochoa. "There is not one in the Southwest who is faster on the draw, or more deadly with his aim."

"I've heard that before," said Ross. "Somewhere, there is a man who is faster and deadlier, and beyond him there is another who is still more faster and more deadly, and so on and so on. . . ."

"He will save this ranch from Newcomb. He will protect Señor Fitzgerald and his sister. He will face down and defeat Hardy Newcomb."

"All that leaves is the devil himself," said Ross. He looked up at the kid. "The *uiboras cascabeles* is stuffin' his gut. He says you should come over there. He wants to talk with you."

The young man smiled. "At once!" he said. He left the bunkhouse.

"Jesus God," said Ross, rolling his eyes upward. "Now we got the Tascosa Kid as Sir Galahad in New Mexico. First thing you know they'll have him in a nursery rhyme, for the little ones who haven't learned to read yet!"

He was still sitting there when he heard Ochoa's voice outside the bunkhouse, and later that of Joe Bacon and another waddie, the older man named Greener. In a few minutes Ochoa came into the bunkhouse and got his rifle. He did not speak to Ross as he left. In a little while Ross heard the beating of hoofs, heading for the gate.

Ross walked to the door and leaned against the side of it. "I wonder if Don Fitzgerald really knows what is going on around here?" he said aloud.

"He will," said a quiet female voice.

Ross turned quickly to look into the face of Maureen Fitzgerald. He snatched off his hat. "I'm sorry," he said.

"I wanted to see how you were," she said.

"I'm fine, ma'am," said Ross hastily.

"Come over to the house with me," she said. "I'd like to clean those wounds. Infection sets in easily."

"No need for that!" said Ross. He remembered too well the odor of sweat and manure that had hung about him the time she had dressed those wounds.

She smiled. "It's an order," she said.

"I don't work here," he said.

"Then come for my sake," she said.

There was no further argument after that. As they walked toward the big casa, they did not see the Tascosa Kid step from the shadows near the cookhouse and look after them. He snatched the cigarette from his lips and stamped on it, then walked toward the stables. Deep in his eyes there was a new and fiercely forbidding light.

CHAPTER TEN

HER HANDS were soft, deft and gentle. Ross again had the problem of keeping his mind on other things while looking directly at her bosom. Begod, he had never had that trouble with Mary Ellen Spragg when he had been courting her in the old days. The intent and the action had been the same thing in those days.

She passed a cool hand along his flushed cheek. "There," she said. "You seem to heal quickly."

"Maybe it's all in the mind," he said.

She smiled. "It's an interesting thought."

"It don't help much when a cow steps on your foot, or a bullet gets poked into your hide," he said.

She shook her head. The firelight brought out the highlights of her hair, and seemed to accentuate the creaminess of her complexion. "You are riding into Las Piedras with Sean, are you not?" she said.

He grinned wryly. "I don't have much choice," he said.

"Sean would not order you to go," she said.

"He didn't. It was something else. He give his word. I can't welsh on that," he lied bravely.

There was a faint amused look on her face. "Would you like sherry or Tokay?" she said.

"I don't go for that foreign booze," said Ross. He flushed. "I didn't mean it the way I said it," he added.

She laughed. "It's wine."

"Brandy will do me fine," he said. "I shouldn't ought'a be drinking in the presence of a lady. My mom told me that when I was a kid. It didn't stop my pa though. He was always boozin' it up around Mom, and *she* was a lady, I tell you, ma'am!"

She filled a glass for him from a cut-glass decanter and

placed it on the table. "It was Tascosa that really made you decide to go to Las Piedras, wasn't it, Ross?"

"He can't make me do nothin'!" said Ross angrily.

"But it's true, isn't it?"

He nodded. "I don't want no trouble with the Kid," he said.

"No one seems to want trouble with him."

"He's a good man for the job your brother gave him. I'll say that for him."

She looked into the fireplace, as though she could see pictures in the dancing flames. "I wonder,". she mused. "Hardy Newcomb is a hard man. He brooks no interference with his way."

"You can say that again," said Ross. He sipped the brandy.

"Are you afraid of him too?"

Ross shrugged. "I'd feel better with a couple of counties between me and him."

"What will happen tomorrow?"

"Your guess is as good as mine, ma'am. I don't have much choice."

"You can still refuse to go."

He shook his head. "I've changed my mind."

"Because of Sean? Or Tascosa?"

"Neither one. I'm sorry I got mixed up in this war, but I ain't goin' to let Hardy Newcomb hammer *his* damned law into me, beggin' your pardon, ma'am."

She sat down and looked at this lean hawk of a man, with the battered face, and the simple, but forthright, ideas. He was almost, but not quite, homely. He had a way of looking directly at one, and she knew he was hard beneath his simple manner; hard enough to kill if he had to, and yet there was something else within him. Something she could not quite define, and yet she knew this hidden quality was something entirely alien to Tascosa. There was more. She felt herself drawn to this lean lobo of a man, and yet she knew there could be nothing between them. They were planets apart. She had assured herself of that a number of times in the darkness of her room, staring up at the ceiling, surrounded by many men, yet utterly alone amongst them.

"You're not in the same room with me, ma'am," he chided gently.

She started. "I'm sorry! I meant to ask you why you had come back to Verde County."

"*Quién sabe?* I was headin' north anyways."

"You came from the Columbus area. That's almost due west, isn't it?"

He flushed. "Not quite."

She smiled. "You came to see Tascosa, didn't you?"

He raised his eyes, and the hard light came into them. "Supposin' I did? It was the biggest mistake I've made in the past few years, and I've made quite a passel of them. I should'a kept goin' north!"

"Where, and to what, Ross?"

He emptied the brandy glass. "My brother has the old family place on the Canadian. I can run it."

"Is that what you really want to do?"

He looked directly at her and something passed between them; something perhaps that neither of them really wanted, or *thought* they didn't want, but it was there between them for the taking. "Ain't much else," he said quietly. He could not bear to look into those eyes, for he had the eerie feeling he would fall into them, deep, deep, and never find his way out of them again. "I'm tired of driftin', fightin', eatin' a Spanish supper and sleepin' in a Spanish bed." He looked quickly at her with that whimsical sideways smile of his. "That last don't quite mean the same like it sounds."

"What does it mean, Ross?"

"A Spanish supper is to tighten your belt a notch and a Spanish bed is to lie face down on the hard ground and pull your back over you for a cover."

She nodded. "You're tired of the old ways; the sowing of wild oats."

"That's it exactly."

She looked into the flames of the fireplace. "You're sure about that?" she asked softly.

It was a picture that would stay in his memory for the rest of his life, but he didn't know it then. She could read his mind. He was sure of it now. "Yes," he lied.

"Then you should have gone directly north to the Canadian, Ross. No, Ross, you are not through with the old ways. Not quite yet. Otherwise you would not have come back to Verde County." She looked directly at him. "It is Tascosa, is it not?"

"I ain't smart enough to figger that one out," he said defensively.

"He is," she said simply.

"Maybe so," he said hotly.

"Where will all this end?"

He looked directly at her. "You know the answer as well as I do, ma'am," he said. He emptied his glass and stood up. "Thanks for your kindness."

She walked with him to the door. She looked up at him in the darkness of the hall. "Please call me Maureen," she said.

"I ain't got that right, ma'am."

For a moment she stood there looking at him and then she touched his battered face with the tips of her fingers. "I'm giving you that right, Ross," she said softly.

The impulse to draw her close swept through him so quickly he almost acted before he thought, and when he did think, it seemed as though his knees were going to betray him. He actually felt as though he was swaying a little on his feet. "Thank you, Maureen," he said huskily.

Something passed between them again, and Ross knew that whatever happened to her present frame of mind, his would never change, and the swiftness and the wonder of it shook him throughout his body and soul.

She had seemed to be waiting for something and when it did not come she touched his arm. "Take care of my brother tomorrow," she said.

"He's supposed to be takin' care of me," he said with a smile.

"Please take care of Tascosa too," she said.

He looked back at the closed door as he walked toward the bunkhouse. "Well, I'll be damned," he said to himself. "She ain't worried about ol' Ross Starkey and his bashed-in phiz. She's just worried about her brother and that damned Tascosa! Man, maybe I ain't too bright at that! She dealt out them cards so fast I never did see her doctor up the deck! Tascosa!" He mimicked her voice. "Please take care of Tascosa too," he simpered. "Bull crap! Like takin' a half-grown grizzly bear to bed with you. Me? I'd sooner have the grizzly at that!"

The ranch area was very quiet. The wind swayed the trees and the brush and it brought the faint music of the river to Ross. The brandy was warm in his lean gut. He lighted a cigarette and looked back at the house. There was one lighted window in the second story. It was her room. He saw the outline of her figure dark against the soft lamplight and once again he was badly shaken. No one had heard his last bitter words, but he knew deep within his heart that it was not so. It couldn't be so!

He lighted the cigarette. The flare of the match revealed his hawk's face and then it was gone. For a moment she stood there and then she drew the drapes across the window. Ross walked slowly toward the bunkhouse. He was too old a hand with the fillies to let any of them break him up. Sure, *he* knew women!

He walked into the empty bunkhouse. He had never seen a corrida that spent more time in the saddle than the "Shamrock" riders, and usually at night too. He hunted down Tascosa's bottle and helped himself. By bedtime he was half-seas over and he didn't give a tinker's damn for Tascosa, Hardy Newcomb and the whole of Verde County, *but he could not erase Maureen Fitzgerald from his mind.*

There had been a lot of comings and goings during the night, with muttered conversations outside of the bunkhouse, none of which had been intelligible to Ross. At dawn his head felt like it was going to burst. After breakfast, as he rode with Sean Fitzgerald and Tascosa along the river road, his face must have revealed how he felt, for the other two were careful not to say anything to him.

When the sun came up the world seemed to silently explode into the dreamlike quality of a New Mexico autumn. The hills had begun to be mantled in scarlet, purple and gold. Green clouds of cottonwoods seemed to float above bronze-red hills. The wind was soft and the air dry and winey, after the rains. White puffs of clouds were conjured up out of thin air by some unseen master magician and they drifted from east to west, increasing in number as the day grew warmer and warmer, while their shadows followed the flow of the rolling land.

It was almost noon when they reached the outskirts of Las Piedras, riding slowly along a winding road, tree-shaded, where adobe after adobe, like beads on a string, lined both sides of the road. Bare-legged children scuttled for cover as *los gringos* rode by. They knew these cold-eyed men who

rode with careless ease and with death hidden in their hol-
sters and saddle scabbards. Many of their families' friends
and relatives had died or been crippled in the periodic and
deadly warfare that swept Verde County in cycles.

Older eyes peered from the secretive windows and from
the tilled fields about the wide valley. They knew two of those
men. It was a partisan country; there was no in-between. Two
of the riding trio were not Newcomb men. One was the
leader of the "Shamrock" corrida, and the young man who
rode beside him was almost a Verde County legend. The
third man they did not know, but he had the stamp of the
gunfighter on him.

The pinnacled rocks that half encircled Las Piedras,
and which had given it its name, were sun-soaked that day,
warm and bronzed in the bright, clear light. Beyond them a
faint bluish haze was already forming on the mountains.
The adobes and jacales of Las Piedras slept in the warm
sunlight, with scarlet *ristras* of peppers like coagulated blood
hanging against the yellow-brown walls. The doors and windows had been painted blue for the most part and here and
there on the walls the sun glinted brightly from shining
stones set into the adobe when it was wet, in the form of the
Cross.

The horses clattered over a bridge that spanned an *acequia
madre*, bringing fresh, clear water to the irrigated fields beyond the town. Cottonwoods and willows waved beside the
acequias, while long-tailed magpies flitted about, at peace
with clouds of smaller birds that seemed to prefer the vicinity
of the houses to the waving trees. The clear, bell-like sound
of meadowlarks came out on the soft wind.

There were other eyes on the three riders as they approached the center of the town. Indolent women looked
sideways from liquid eyes, and it was at the tallest of the
riders they looked, while their men folk peered warily from
beneath their wide hat brims, brown hands feeling for knife
hilts. The object of the looks from both sexes rode loose
and easy in the saddle, cigarette hanging from the side of his
mouth, as though he was not in enemy country. The Kid
was drinking it all in.

They rode into the *placita* and tethered their horses in
front of the sheriff's office, beside the adobe *calabozo*. Eyes
peered between the rusted bars of the cell windows and nar-

rowed as they saw Tascosa. Here and there about the sun-soaked plaza men shifted their positions. Others looked through the windows of the saloons. There was an unusual absence of women and children about the plaza, but there were many horses, most of them with the Newcomb Box HN brand on them, tethered to the hitching racks.

Sean Fitzgerald dismounted. He looked about. "I don't like the looks of this," he said.

Tascosa dismounted and fashioned a cigarette, watching the lounging men across the *placita*. "Everything will be all right," he said. He looked at Ross. "There are your three sparring partners from Santo Tomas."

Ross nodded. He had already seen the three of them standing beneath the wooden awning of a saloon three doors down from the sheriff's office. He looked back the way he and the others had just come. There had been no Newcomb men in sight as they had approached the center of Las Piedras; now he could see four men leaning against adobes on either side of the street mouth. He mentally cursed himself for not pulling leather the night before. "Time for a drink," he said. "My *cabeza* is killin' me."

Sean Fitzgerald shook his head. "Not yet," he said.

Tascosa opened the door of the sheriff's office and bowed a little as he ushered the others in. Ross looked sideways at the Kid; the sonofabitch was as cool as a brass monkey's butt in the winter time. Ross had to give him credit for that, at least.

Dan Hurley looked up from his desk. Hardy Newcomb straddled a chair backward, his thick forearms resting on the chair back, his hat level above his level brows, his thick mustache level above the narrow line of his level mouth. He looked like a damned heathen Chinee joss idol sitting there, thought Ross.

"I see you kept your word," said Hurley with his usual smooth smile. Everything about Dan Hurley was smooth, except, perhaps, his conscience, but only he and God would know about that.

Fitzgerald nodded. "Mister Starkey kept his word as well."

"He did?" said Newcomb. "I could have sworn he'd be crossing the Tres Cerros by now."

Ross felt for the makings. The old coot was right at that

—Ross *would* be, if Tascosa hadn't outsmarted—or out-bluffed—Ross, whichever way you looked at it.

Newcomb and Tascosa looked at each other and neither of them looked away, and neither of them would, as though the older bull of the herd, still powerful and still in command, were taking the measure of his possible successor. Ross wondered idly what kind of a young man Hardy Newcomb had been. He had a pretty good idea. He had one advantage on Tascosa; he had lived a good part of his allotted span.

Fitzgerald took off his hat and brushed back his fine blond hair. "All you have against Mister Starkey is circumstantial evidence, Sheriff Hurley, and none of it very good at that."

"We'll be the judge of that," said Newcomb.

"I'll just bet you will," said Tascosa.

"As I see it," said Fitzgerald. "Mister Starkey was in Boca Grande when the stolen cattle were driven through it. He left the canyon, pursued by some of Mister Newcomb's riders, leaving his hat behind."

"He sure did," said Newcomb. It was about as close as he'd come to a joke.

"You have no proof he was with the men who took the cattle. You don't even know who they were. You have no case at all against Mister Starkey," said the rancher.

"The sheriff is going to hold him under suspicion," said Newcomb.

Ross felt cold inside. He remembered all too well how many of the Newcomb corrida were lounging about the *placita,* waiting, just *waiting.*

Tascosa rolled a fresh smoke. He leaned indolently against the wall, watching the others, now and then looking through the dusty glass of the window.

"I protest," said Fitzgerald.

"You crap," said Newcomb heavily. He stood up.

Hurley flushed. He was too much of the politician to stand for all of Newcomb's blunt, undiplomatic ways. "I'll have to keep him, Mister Fitzgerald," he said.

"I'll put up his bail," said the rancher.

Hurley waved a smooth hand. "He is held without bail. Incommunicado," he said.

Tascosa smiled. "What's that? Without toilet privileges?"

Hurley looked at the Kid. "Sometimes you annoy me," he said.

"The feeling is mutual."

"You're a long way from your manure pile, Kid," said Newcomb. "Whyn't you go and strut in front of the hens? You're damned good at that, they tell me."

Boots popped on the boardwalk in front of the office and the door swung open. An elderly man looked at Newcomb. "Damnedest thing, boss," he said breathlessly. "Them cows that was run off out'a Boca Grande Canyon is right back there, grazin' as peaceful as you please."

"You sure, Marty?" said Newcomb.

"Positive, boss. You know me."

Newcomb nodded. He looked at Ross. "That still don't clear you in *my* book," he said.

Ross felt a chill. His bootheels felt like they wanted to sprout wings.

"Then you have no reason to hold Mister Starkey?" said Fitzgerald.

Hurley looked at Newcomb. Newcomb shook his head. Hurley turned, like a puppet, and smiled. "No," he said.

Tascosa walked to the door and opened it. Sean Fitzgerald had a puzzled look on his face as he walked outside into the bright sunlight. Ross looked curiously at Tascosa. The Kid's face was a blank. Tascosa shut the door behind him. "You want that drink now, amigo?" he said.

Ross felt for the makings. He could see the Newcomb men still idling about the *placita*. His three sparring partners, as Tascosa had called them were still standing there, looking directly at the three "Shamrock" men. "I think we ought to get the hell out'a here, *if* we can," he said.

"They won't start anything," said Fitzgerald. "You're freed of those charges, Ross."

"Yeh," said Ross. "We know that, but do *they?*"

The door opened behind them and Hardy Newcomb came out. He was lighting a cigar. He looked over the flare of the match directly into Ross' eyes. "You can leave," he said dryly.

"Gracias," said the Kid. "God has spoken. Everything is all right now."

Newcomb fanned out the match, never taking his eyes from the Kid. He worked the cigar from one side of his mouth to the other. It was as though he was measuring Tascosa in infinite detail, leaving nothing to chance or hearsay, as though he was impressing every feature of the man on an indelible page in his mental files.

Ross mounted and waited for the others.

Tascosa looked up at Ross. "How about that drink?" he said.

"Suddenly I ain't thirsty," said Ross.

Sean Fitzgerald untethered his horse. "I think we had better leave," he said.

Tascosa shrugged. He mounted and the three of them rode slowly from the *placita,* under the cold, level eyes of Newcomb's men.

It wasn't until they were well clear of the town that Ross turned in his saddle and looked back. They were not being followed, but it was still a long way to the Rio Dulces.

Sean Fitzgerald took out his cigar case and passed it first to Tascosa and then to Ross. After all three of them lighted up, he looked back toward Las Piedras as Ross had done. "You know," he said thoughtfully, "it was almost as though Hardy Newcomb expected that to happen."

Ross blew out a puff of smoke. The thought had occurred to him too. "He plays a deep game," he said.

Tascosa blew a smoke ring and punched a finger through it. "He ain't so damned smart as he thinks he is," he said. He grinned secretively.

"What do you mean by that?" asked Fitzgerald.

Tascosa shook his head. "Nothing, sir, absolutely nothing."

Fitzgerald flushed. "You go out of your way to antagonize that man," he said quietly. "I won't stand for much more of it, Tascosa. I have too much to take into consideration. I have written to the new governor for help in this harassment I have been suffering from Newcomb. Let's do this thing my way."

"And get a bullet in the back?" sneered Tascosa. "The new governor won't do anything about it. He knows who runs Verde County. He knows where the votes come from."

"He's appointed by the Federal government, isn't he?" said the rancher.

"Sure, sure, but most of the rest of the Territorial officials are elected. They control most of the money in this Territory and don't you ever forget it, and they can put pressure on Washington to make or break a governor. They won't buck up against Hardy Newcomb. That was a fool thing to do, writing to Santa Fe."

"It's my way," said Fitzgerald defensively. "What do you think, Ross?"

Ross took the cigar from his mouth. "I say a man should fight for his land. It don't have to be with bullets, though."

"Hear, hear," jeered Tascosa.

Ross jammed the cigar back into his mouth. Tascosa had a great way of rubbing salt into a person's feeling, the egotistical sonofabitch. "Please take care of Tascosa too," she had said. Ross would like to take care of him all right, but not the way she had meant him to.

Ross glanced at the Kid, riding jauntily, cigar poked up at an angle like a bowstaff on a river steamer, satisfied with himself of course, but not quite satisfied with the world— although, of course, he meant to change all that. Sure, Hardy Newcomb had seemed to know that those cattle had been returned, but there also had seemed to be something else up his sleeve besides his arm. Something that neither of the "Shamrock" men suspected, but Ross had an uncanny, uneasy feeling, and he wouldn't rest well until he found out what it was, although he wasn't sure he really wanted to know.

They reached the valley of the Rio Dulces in the middle of the afternoon. Fitzgerald smiled. "It's beautiful," he said. He looked at Ross. "You're sure you won't stay with us?"

Ross shook his head. "Hardy Newcomb ain't forgave me," he said. "He ain't about to, neither. He don't ever forget a man once he's done something Hardy Newcomb don't like. He's got his sights on me. I make one false move in this county and he'll get me one way or another."

Tascosa laughed. "You goin' to let that old hellion scare you away?"

Ross looked at him. "Yes," he said simply. "I got no war with him."

Tascosa yawned. *"You* called *me* yella last night," he said.

Fitzgerald looked at Ross and then at Tascosa. "Maybe it is best that you leave, Ross," he said.

"I'm goin'," said Ross. "Ain't no question about that."

They rode down the long slope. Shadows were gathering on

the eastern slopes of the broken hills. A cool wind picked its
way up the valley of the Rio Dulces. It was quiet and peaceful,
and yet there was something haunting the oncoming dusk.
Something that had not yet shown its ugly mask.

CHAPTER ELEVEN

THE WEATHER had changed, driving away the mild sunny days with their cool, dry winds, to replace them with an intense heat that filled even the otherwise cool valleys. The sun beat down on the range, ravaging it once more before the start of the true fall weather.

Ross Starkey broke his simple camp on a fork of the Rio Dulces. He had left the "Shamrock" ranch two days before, after making his goodbyes to the Fitzgeralds. Tascosa had vanished, riding forth with half a dozen of the hardcases that had drifted to the Rio Dulces country to ride under the Tascosa Kid. Ross had intended to ride to the western slopes of the mountains and then strike across the Jornada del Muerto to the Rio Grande and then take it by easy stages north to Albuquerque and eventually to Santa Fe. He wanted to see his brother Lloyd. Lloyd had always been the cool head in his family, the steadfast reliable type who had left the ranch on the Canadian to work for his law degree, taking care of his aging mother as well, while Ross had drifted through the years, always looking for the pot at the end of the rainbow. So far it had cost him some of the best years of his life, and the future didn't look much better from where Ross sat his horse. Maybe Lloyd would have the answers.

Still, it wasn't easy to leave the Rio Dulces country. He had grown to like and respect Sean Fitzgerald, as Tascosa had done. The Irishman was everything that Ross wasn't, and the same thing could be said about the Kid, except that the Kid had an intense, though perhaps warped, loyalty to the rancher, which might have in it the seeds of doom for Sean Fitzgerald.

He had said goodbye to Maureen, with her brother standing

close by and Tascosa in the offing, so there was nothing that could be said openly. After he had left her he had thought of wonderful things he could have said, that would have painted a masterpiece of his feeling toward her, but the words had not come at the right time. Once again the hag of loneliness had returned to Ross Starkey, and this time it was more bitter than gall.

A man leaves a part of himself wherever he goes. Bit by bit his body and soul are invisibly chipped at and eroded by life, and many times a man leaves something behind that years later comes back to haunt him. For some reason or another, there are scales before his eyes at the time. There is one thing sure: in almost every case, he can never return to that distant time. This time Ross had experienced something, and had known at the time it was something he had never experienced before. He had left part of himself, perhaps the greatest part of himself, in the cool deft hands and deep eyes of Maureen Fitzgerald. The rest was a husk. Just dross. A mechanical man.

The sun beat down into the windless canyons, filling them with a heat and glare that seemed to bounce from the drying ground, to strike into a man's face even beneath his low-pulled hat brim and strike deep into his eyes. Ross couldn't hurry, despite the desire to escape the heat and the glare. Each stride of the claybank was carrying him farther and farther away from the Rio Dulces and Maureen Fitzgerald. He couldn't hurry, and yet he knew he had to go.

The late afternoon heat caught him as he crossed a ridge in the full light of the sun. He wiped the sweat from his face and urged the claybank down toward the shade of the trees. He began to fashion a smoke as he reached the trees. Here and there, further up the canyon he could see scattered clumps of "Shamrock" cattle. The mouth of the canyon debouched onto sloping land that led down toward Newcomb's Box HN range. A stout fence had been built across the mouth of the canyon and he could just see it from where he sat his horse.

He lighted the cigarette and flipped the match into the fork. As he did so he saw black shapes silhouetted against the startling blue of the cloudless sky. They were wheeling lower and lower and every now and then one of them would drop out of sight just beyond the fence. Ross blew a puff of smoke. Likely a dead cow over there, or maybe a dead jack-rabbit. He leaned on his saddlehorn and watched the wheeling buzzards. One good thing about the ugly devils, they sure cleaned up the range in a hurry.

One by one the buzzards landed, but one of them still swung about against the blue, like a charred newspaper being lifted by the wind, only there wasn't any wind. Maybe they kept a guard up, thought Ross. It's a cinch no man was about, for those buzzards would rise like a filthy cloud and circle patiently, somehow knowing the exact range of the man's rifle, and hovering just beyond it.

Ross rode along the fork. He didn't want to go near New-comb's Box HN range, but he had to follow the fence line or cross those damned heat-blasted hills, and even Hardy Newcomb couldn't panic Ross into doing that, not this day at any rate.

He saw the buzzards in a mass just beyond the fence line, waddling in, poking their ugly naked necks into the carrion they had found, ripping and tearing with beaks as strong as a blacksmith's pincers. He eyed with disgust their dusty black feathers. Christ, but they were really at it!

He saw part of the carrion as he reached the fence. It was a steer, a small one from his sight of it. Maybe a yearling. It wasn't much bigger than a man. The buzzards hadn't caught Ross' scent as yet, although the lone one in the sky was swinging over, with motionless pinions, rising and falling easily on the hot updraft from the naked hills.

Ross kneed the claybank away from the fence. He had caught the sweet-rotten odor of decaying flesh. He threw away his cigarette in disgust. Even the weed seemed to smell and taste of the carrion. He felt for the full bottle of rye in a saddlebag, parting gift of Sean Fitzgerald. Maybe a slug would take the taste out of his dry mouth and throat. He drank deeply and drove the cork back into the bottle. As he did so the buzzards caught wind of him. Squawking and protesting, they waddled along the dusty ground, rising heavily and sluggishly into the air, flapping off toward the hills, leaving behind the torn and dusty carrion.

Ross glanced once more at the carrion and drew rein sharply. He narrowed his eyes. It was the damnedest-looking fallen hide he had ever seen. No legs, just a long sort of dusty, ripped cylinder, with the dusty head in plain view.

Ross leaned forward in the saddle and stared at it. The damned booze was working fast, *for it seemed as though the head was looking back at him!*

Ross wiped the sweat from his face. He shook his head. It must be the enervating heat and the booze. He looked at the carrion again and a ghastly feeling came over him. Slowly he slid from the saddle and walked to the fence, staring at the carrion. He pushed up a strand of the cruel barbed wire and shoved down on the one below it with his foot, working his way through, heedless of a barb that raked his broad back. He walked slowly toward the carrion, his spurs ringing softly in the dust.

Ross stopped and put his hand to his mouth. Suddenly he spun about and heaved his liquor, followed by his last meal, then followed by pure bile. His strength drained from him, and he stood there, spraddle-legged, head bent low, chest and gut heaving, with strings of slimy green hanging from his widespread mouth. "Jesus, oh Jesus," he gasped. He passed a hard hand across his streaming eyes. The smell of the carrion seemed to drift around him but his gut was empty.

He turned slowly and looked about. The range was empty, heat shimmering in the sun, seeming to rise and fall. The buzzards were high up now, so high it hurt to look up at them in that bright sky, swinging in great, lazy circles, waiting for the live man-smell to stop spoiling their meal.

Ross looked at the head that protruded from the ripped green hide, but the eyes were gone and the tongue that had protruded from the blackened mouth had been eaten away to the roots. The white teeth were shown in a perpetual grin, for the soft puffed lips had also been eaten away, while harsh beaks had already torn into the flesh of the cheeks. The booted feet, the spurs red-scaled with fresh rust, were tied at the ankles, protruding from the shrunken hide like the twin flippers of a seal.

Ross wiped his mouth. He had heard of such things, but had never seen anything like it. The Comanches practiced such an agonizing method of execution, lashing the victim in a fresh buffalo hide, head and feet protruding from it, then placing the screaming, half-mad victim under the blazing sun. The sun would slowly constrict the green hide like the coils of a python, until the eyes protruded and the swollen tongue was pushed through the out-thrust, blackened lips. Sometimes the buzzards got there before the victim was dead. . . .

Ross looked about again. There was no sign of life except for the buzzards, now almost indistinguishable against the glare of the sun. He forced himself to walk to the side of the victim. The man had been slight of build, dark-haired and -mustached. A queer feeling came over Ross. He drew out his clasp knife and opened the big blade. He gathered all his will power and began to slit the rawhide lashings that bound the dead man inside the green hide. He forced himself to push a shaking hand inside and feel for the man's wallet. He withdrew it. He opened the stinking thing, trying to keep his internal organs inside his gut, for he knew they'd be next if he heaved again. There was nothing else left to heave.

He opened the wallet in the full light of the sun. A picture fluttered to the ground. He picked it up and looked at it, seeing the rather rounded and stupid face of a young woman, hardly more than a girl. He turned it over. "To Francisco with all my love," he said in Spanish. A horrible feeling came over him again. He now suspected the truth, but he didn't want to face it. He poked through the few papers in the wallet. He closed it and placed it inside his shirt. There wasn't any doubt about it now. The carrion was all that was left of Francisco Ochoa. In following his idol, the Tascosa Kid, he had followed the last trail out.

Ross got a blanket from his horse. He rolled the stiffened corpse, green hide and all, into it, then carried it to the horse. The claybank shied and blowed repeatedly, backing away from the stench until Ross belted him once or twice atop the head. Ross lashed the corpse on the claybank.

He rolled and lighted a cigarette, looking back across the Box HN range. It was as deserted as before. The buzzards were gone in search of another meal. Ross looked at a distant motte. There was a bright flash, as though the sun had reflected on polished metal, and for a second or two his hair rose on the back of his neck, as he awaited a rifle bullet. He trotted toward the woods along the fork and led the claybank into the hot shade.

Maybe he hadn't been destined to leave the "Shamrock" and the Rio Dulces country; not quite yet, anyway.

The sun was gone when he topped the last broken hill that lay between him and the Rio Dulces Valley. Far down below him he could see the ranch buildings within their screen of dark greenery. A streamer of smoke rose high above the buildings in the windless air. There was a faint stirring and movement of the atmosphere as the heat of the day began to be dissipated by the cool of the evening.

He limped a little as he led the claybank down the darkening slopes. He had gotten accustomed to the stench of the swollen, mutilated corpse, but it had cost him half the bottle of rye and two sacks of Dime Durham to do it. It was a helluva gift he was bringing back to the ranch. He remembered all too well, almost as though it was yesterday, seeing the older Ochoa, Diego by name, writhing and screaming in the bloody dust until a bullet in the gaping mouth had stopped his screaming forever. He had been a good man to ride the *rio* with, a boon companion and a fighter from whom had laid the chunk, but the Seven Rivers corrida had wiped the slate almost clean in their ambush, and Diego Ochoa had been one of those who had helped pay the butcher's bill. Somehow or another, Francisco seemed also to have died in the same cause, if one could call it that. To Ross, both killings had been senseless.

He tethered the claybank to a rear fence, out of scent of the house. He limped through the darkness, cigarette hanging from his mouth.

"Stand where you are!" a hard voice said.

"It's Starkey," said another voice. It was Mac McArthur.

Ross shoved back his sweat-damp hat. "Where's the Kid?" he said.

"In the bunkhouse," said Mac.

"Tell him I want to see him."

The other man laughed. "You go see *him*, Starkey. I ain't about to tell him to come see you." He spat to one side. "He ain't feelin' too kindly toward you, anyways."

"The feeling is mutual, Nelson," said Ross dryly.

"Don't rile him," said Mac. "He's been like a boogered grizzly all day. Been lookin' for Francisco."

"I found him," said Ross.

"Where is he?"

"Go get the Kid," said Ross.

Charley Nelson walked to the bunkhouse and called inside. In a moment the broad shoulders of the Kid filled the lamplighted doorway of the bunkhouse. "That you, Ross?" he called out in a cold voice. "They say you found Francisco. Is he all right?"

"Come and see."

"Dammit! Don't play cute with me! Where is he?"

Ross turned on a heel and walked to the claybank. He led the tired horse through a narrow gateway and then toward the three men.

"God's sake, Starkey," said Nelson. "You ought to change them drawers of yourn once in a while, anyways."

"That ain't Starkey," said Mac in a faraway voice. He looked sideways at the Kid.

Tascosa walked forward. "What the hell is this?" he said.

Ross took out his clasp knife and cut loose the lashings, heedless of the fine reata he was completely ruining. He forced himself to take the stiffened body from the horse and carry it toward the light streaming from the bunkhouse doorway. He placed it on the hard-packed earth and then looked at the Kid. "Take a look," he said in an expressionless voice.

Someone came through the darkness from the casa. "Who is it, Tascosa?" called out Sean Fitzgerald.

Tascosa stood looking down at the blanket-shrouded form.

"It's Ross Starkey, Mister Fitzgerald," said Nelson.

"I thought you had left," said Fitzgerald.

"I had to come back," said Ross.

Tascosa pulled back the blanket from the horrible head of the young New Mexican. "Jesus God!" he said. He slapped a hand over his mouth and nose and staggered backward.

"It's Francisco Ochoa," said Ross. "I found him near the east mouth of Boca Grande, just beyond your ranch line, Mister Fitzgerald." He looked at the rancher. "Somebody lashed him inside a green hide and left him under the sun a coupla days. The buzzards got to him before I found him. . . ."

"Why? Why?" said Fitzgerald.

"Ask Tascosa," said Ross quietly.

Tascosa turned. "What the hell do you mean, Starkey?"

"You know as well as I do what some men do to rustlers, Kid. You haven't forgotten Print Olive, have you? Seems to me you said you had ridden for him once, or was that some more of your bullshit?"

"Don't you talk to me that way!"

"Somebody has to," said Ross. "It looks like it's up to me."

"Who's Print Olive?" said Fitzgerald in a puzzled tone.

"Toughest old boot in the Southwest," said Mac. "If he caught a man on his range, foolin' with his cows, he'd kill the nearest cow and strip the hide from it, then lash the rustler into it, leaving him out in the sun. Sometimes they lasted a coupla days, but not often."

"I can't believe it!" said the rancher.

Ross turned. "Dammit!" he snapped. "You're lookin' at it!"

"Don't talk to Mister Fitzgerald like that!" warned the Kid.

Ross turned toward him. "You had them cows run off from the Box HN," he said quietly. "But *you* wasn't there. You sent Francisco and some of the others to drive them cows back onto the Box HN to make Hardy Newcomb look like a damned fool. Well, you only *think* you done it. You ain't smart enough to beat Newcomb at his own game. He knew those cows had come back. He also knew what had happened to Francisco. You stood there in Hurley's office matching looks with Newcomb and acting like you was king of the manure pile. Well you was and you are, you short-sighted, conceited, lying sonofabitch!"

Tascosa dropped his hand to his Colt, but he was a mite too late, for once in his life. Ross hit him with a long, stabbing left and followed through with a right hook that sent the tall man reeling into Nelson and McArthur.

"Keep your hands from that gun!" snapped Fitzgerald to the Kid.

For one white-hot second Ross thought he was going to get a softnosed .44/40 in his empty gut, and then the Kid shook his head to get the blood-glare out of his eyes. He slowly wiped the blood from his mouth and smiled over his hand at Ross. Then he unbuckled his gunbelt and handed the finely tooled leather, heavy with the engraved Colt and bright brass cartridges, to Nelson.

Ross unbuckled his gunbelt and dropped the gear on the hard ground, careless of the Colt. He raised his fists. The Kid came forward on cat feet, stabbing out with a long left, gauging Ross, and when he threw his right it went clean over Ross' left forearm and hit just below his left eye, stinging like a nettle. The right struck his chin and rocked him backward. The Kid laughed, forcing the fight, throwing smooth punches that stabbed and rocked Ross like a perfectly timed pile driver. Then out of nowhere a right caught the Kid on the button and a left smashed into his lean gut, followed by a short right uppercut that drove him back against the bunkhouse wall. Something fell to the floor inside the building.

Ross took two stinging punches to get in between the Kid's flailing arms. He kept bouncing the Kid from the wall, meeting him with thudding blows, until the Kid squirmed free, gasping for air, dancing about, blowing blood from his handsome nose. He grinned through the blood and sweat, but Ross knew he had shaken the Kid.

"Time!" said Fitzgerald.

"Time, shit!" said Ross. He rushed the taller man.

They stood toe to toe, driving in unscientific punches, neither of them giving or taking an inch until Ross drove the Kid back.

"Stay away from him, Kid!" yelled Baldy the cook from the cookhouse. He ran out waving a skillet.

The Kid did stay away from Ross, bobbing and weaving, but in so doing, he couldn't quite get the range of the bloody-faced man who stalked him like a lobo wolf, taking soft punches to drive those rock-hard fists into gut and jaw, until the Kid went down hard, lying flat on his back looking up into Ross' bloody face with pure hell in his eyes.

"Enough," said the rancher.

"Enough, hell!" said the Kid. He got slowly to his feet, but hadn't set himself when that damned drifter bored in again, smashing and slamming, ramming his head against the Kid's jaw while he hammered at the Kid's ribs. A lucky uppercut snapped Ross' head back and a knee in the crotch bent him forward. The Kid coupled his hands and smashed them down on the back of Ross' neck as he fell, Ross seeing the hard ground coming up to meet his battered face and unable to do a damned thing about it. The impact was even worse than he had expected.

The Kid booted Ross twice before he could roll free.

"Unfair! Unfair!" cried out the rancher.

Ross gripped one of Tascosa's kicking legs and set himself

and came up on his feet, spraddle-legged, and upended the Kid against the rancher. The Kid cursed but a vicious boot took some of the fight out of him and a hard, hooked heel caught him on the side of the jaw. He tried twice to get up and then he lay flat, eyes glazed, dark blood leaking from his gasping mouth.

Ross wiped the blood from his face. He licked his abraded knuckles, looking down at the Kid with dullness in his eyes. The left eye was almost shut by now.

The Kid rolled over and heaved. He pushed his bloody hands against the ground and then fell heavily. The second try worked and he came slowly to his feet, turning quickly with a double-barreled derringer in his right hand, the twin muzzles not three feet from Ross' gut. Ross felt his stomach draw tight, expectant of two softnosed .41 slugs that would rip him wide open to the backbone. For a long, long moment the Kid stood there and then he slowly lowered the skimpy gun. He wiped the blood from his mouth with his free hand. "I guess I owed you that," he said.

"You won't bring that kid back," said Ross.

They stood there face to face, and somehow Ross remembered another scene, fraught with emotion, not too many weeks ago, when Ross had lain on the ground, horseless, weak to the point of utter defeat, waiting for the Kid to kill him for his own benefit so that the Apaches would not get him. He remembered all too well that if Tascosa had not taken him out of that moonlit canyon of impending death he would not be facing the Kid now.

"Shake hands, men," said Fitzgerald.

They still stood there looking at each other, and then Tascosa turned and walked toward the cookhouse.

Ross picked up his gunbelt and swung it about his lean waist with practiced ease. He looked at the rancher. "You'd better bury the kid," he said. "He won't keep in this weather." He limped toward the claybank.

"Well, I'll be damned," said Charley Nelson.

Sean Fitzgerald walked to Ross. He placed a hand on his shoulder. "Don't leave now," he said. "I want to talk with you."

Ross rested his head on the sweat-damp saddle. His bones seemed too soft and pliable to carry him on. His belly felt like mush.

"Just tonight," said the rancher.

Ross nodded. He had lost something again; something he could not name, but it was something he had found in a stinking cell in El Corralitos so many weeks past, and had followed all the way to the Rio Dulces, only to find it turn to ashes in his dry mouth.

CHAPTER TWELVE

THE WEATHER had stayed hot just long enough to help in the horrible death of Francisco Ochoa, but the very night of the day he was laid to rest a storm broke across the mountains. The Thunder People thudded their mad drums in the canyons and across the dark mountains, while eerie sheet lightning flickered bluish tongues of light across the black sky. A wind came up some time before the dawn and brought with it sheets of rain that swept the country with a liquid broom from the Pecos westward across the mountains to the Rio Grande in successive blinding sheets that filled the watercourses brim-full and then flowed over their banks.

In the watery light of dawn, under a lowering sky that seemed to pour forth an unlimited and endless stream of rain, the Rio Dulces swirled over its banks, flooding the bottoms, carrying on its roaring waters the carcasses of drowned cattle, coyotes, rabbits and the writhing bodies of half-drowned snakes, all intermingled with brush and tree trunks, while from beneath the roaring, silty waters came the rumbling of the rocks and stones being carried in the liquid grip of the powerful current, deeply scouring the bed of the river.

Just before noon a thoroughly drenched rider, mud-splashed from head to foot, brought the news that Hardy Newcomb's dam on the Little Bonita had broken during the night. It was a little late to help Fitzgerald's sawmill, for it had been moved to a fork of the Rio Dulces, but the rider also said that the sawmill had more than enough water to turn the heavy machinery, and that Buck Ellwood had sent word that he was ready to try out the new set-up and was only waiting for the ranch owner to come and see it.

Ross Starkey rode with the rancher. He wanted no part of

the ranch, and less of Tascosa, but Fitzgerald was deeply worried, uncertain of himself, and seemed to want someone to talk with besides his ranch hands and his sister.

They rode through the dripping woods on the narrow road that followed the course of the Rio Dulces. Ross was hard put to see out of his left eye. He hadn't seen the Kid since the fight, but he was willing to bet the Kid didn't look any better than Ross did, and maybe worse.

"That was a close thing when the Kid drew on you," said the rancher. "I didn't know he carried a hideout gun, as you Americans call it."

Ross nodded. "Most of them do. It's a handy thing as a last resort."

"Do you carry one?"

"Used to. They took it away from me at El Corralitos. There have been a few times since then that I wished I still had it."

"I wonder what stopped him," mused Fitzgerald.

"You did."

"I didn't say a word."

"No, but you were there."

Fitzgerald turned in his saddle and looked directly at Ross. "You mean that if I hadn't been there he would have killed you in cold blood?"

"Quién sabe? Anyways, it wasn't exactly cold blood."

"It's hard to believe."

Ross shifted in his saddle. "No man can make the Kid lose face. It's part of his very life, Mister Fitzgerald. No one can do it, and I mean absolutely *no* one, exceptin' maybe you. I wouldn't be too sure about that either."

"You're a strange pair. You seem to need each other for some unfathomable reason. Maybe because you're much alike and yet so much unlike each other."

"That's a plain statement," said Ross dryly. "Now tell me what it means."

Fitzgerald shrugged. "Opposites attract, it is said. Maybe that's why he likes me and will do almost anything for me."

"Where does that put me? Like you? That's the best one I've heard in a long time."

"You might have hit it on the head without knowing it, Ross. The Kid admires you for something. Something he lacks. It's pretty obvious why he likes me. He thinks of me as being the sort of gentleman he'd like to be, I suppose. Strangely enough, I admire him for his skill with weapons and horses and as a leader of men, and for his cool courage and his devil-may-care attitude."

"Bravo," said Ross. "Those are fine words for the best killer in Verde County, and maybe all New Mexico Territory."

Fitzgerald nodded. "I've written another letter to the new governor," he said. He looked at Ross. "I want someone to deliver it for me. Someone who can give the governor the additional information he needs on the situation here in Verde County."

"Like me?"

"Like you," agreed the rancher. "Will you do it?"

"Why me?"

Fitzgerald turned in his saddle and looked back through the dripping woods. "I know of no one else I can trust."

"What about Tascosa?"

The rancher shook his head. "The Kid has brought his *own* fight here to the Rio Dulces. I needed his help several years ago and without it I would have been driven from Verde County. It was peaceful for a time until Newcomb got his hackles up again. The Kid seemed to have been sent by a guardian angel to help me, but this time it is different. I want his help, and yet I am afraid to accept it."

"You've done that already," said Ross.

"Maybe I ought to get rid of him?"

Ross glanced sideways at Fitzgerald. "You goin' to tell him that?"

"I'm not afraid of him," said Fitzgerald.

"Maybe not, but I wouldn't ever take a bet, at high odds, which way the Kid was goin' to jump. They say love can easily turn to hate, and the dividing line ain't much."

"You talk like a philosopher."

Ross grinned. "I don't know whether that's a compliment or an insult. What the hell is a philosopher, anyways?"

"A lover of wisdom," said the rancher quietly.

"*Bueno!* I thought maybe it was one of them hombres that made up prescriptions in a drugstore."

The mill appeared through the trees, on a cleared area on the fork of the Rio Dulces, set high enough to be above flood waters, but with the overshot wheel set beneath a solid-looking masonry dam that was overflowing. The great wheel was practically spinning on its axis.

"Wonder that durned wheel don't go flyin' off," said Ross.

"Buck Ellwood knows his business," said the rancher. He looked at Ross. "Will you take the letter?"

Ross felt for the makings. He began to fashion a cigarette.

Fitzgerald moved closer to Ross. "If anything should happen to me, Maureen would lose everything. I have to think of her now, not of myself. Would you do it for her?"

Ross lighted the cigarette. "Ain't nothing goin' to happen to you," he said.

"I have a premonition, Ross. There is information in that letter that can thoroughly incriminate Hardy Newcomb and Dan Hurley. It's only fair to warn you that they'd do anything to keep that information from reaching the hands of the governor."

"I had a feeling it wasn't just goin' to be a joyride," said Ross dryly.

"If anything happens to me, Maureen will give you the letter."

"Ain't nothin' goin' to happen to you!" said Ross hotly.

They crossed the rude bridge. Water was flowing a foot deep over it and they could feel it shaking in the grip of the current.

A slightly built man stood under the dripping eaves of the porch that had been in front of the mill door. He wore a faded blue caped army overcoat. He smiled when he saw the rancher. "I'm glad you came, sir," he said. "Can't do any work in this downpour but it's a good chance to run the machinery. I can make any final adjustments, and as soon as the roads dry out we'll be cutting timber."

They dismounted. "This is Ross Starkey," said the rancher. "Ross, meet Buck Ellwood."

The millman thrust out a left hand. He smiled. "Sorry, I left my right arm at Chickamauga, Starkey," he said.

"Your left feels strong enough for two hands," said Ross.

"The loss of one makes the other compensate, or so they say. Me, I'd rather have two weak ones than one strong one, but the Lord didn't see fit to make it that way." There was nothing sanctimonious in the way he said it. It was simply the statement of a deeply religious man.

Ross led the horses to the shed behind the mill. The rain

had finally stopped. Ross peeled off his slicker and hung it over his saddle. He walked back into the mill and listened to Ellwood as he explained the changes and adjustments he had made in the somewhat aging machinery. Sean Fitzgerald seemed to be fascinated by it. Ross listened for a time, then made himself comfortable in the back of the mill on some baled hay. Fitzgerald had a great future in the Valley of the Rio Dulces, *if* he could settle his war with Hardy Newcomb, but Newcomb was kingpin in that country. He had liked Fitzgerald's money, but as soon as he had realized that the Irishman might rise to a position of wealth and power in the county, he had set his sights on him to bring him down. There could be only one major figure in Verde County, and the position was already taken. There was no room for competitors or usurpers.

Ross had dozed off. Something made him open his eyes. The millman and the rancher were at the back of the mill, beneath some of the machinery. Ross could just hear their voices but he could not make out any of the words. He yawned and rolled over. He felt for the makings and realized he had used up the last sack. He had a couple of sacks of Dime Durham in one of his saddlebags. He walked toward a side door and opened it. Suddenly he stopped. He heard voices again, but they weren't coming from within the mill. Ross stepped outside and stood against the wall beneath the porch roof that rounded the front of the mill and continued along the back to butt onto the shed. He peered around the corner. Half a dozen horses stood in a group and a slickered man stood there holding the reins, a wreath of cigarette smoke rising about his head.

Ross looked further along the bank of the fork. Five men stood beside the dam, their backs toward him, looking at the overflowing dam and the whirling wheel, talking and pointing to the dam and the wheel. Ross studied them. He couldn't tell who they were, but as far as he knew no "Shamrock" men were supposed to be around the mill. One of the men turned and looked at the mill and Ross felt a cold feeling in his gut. It was Art Cassidy. The tall man next to him must be Slim and beyond them, right at the edge of the racing flood, was Ben Miller.

Ross looked back over his shoulder. His Winchester was on his saddle, but to get into the shed he'd pass into view of the horse-holder. He looked back at the mill's side door. Fitzgerald didn't carry a gun and he had seen no belt gun on Ellwood, and with his one arm he could hardly be of much value with a rifle.

He saw one of the men place a blasting powder can beside the dam. He knew well enough what they planned. It would be mighty slick to blow the dam and to ruin the wheel, putting the blame on the storm and the high water. They had missed one thing: they evidently thought there was no one at the mill in this weather; both "Shamrock" horses were in the shed.

Ross had to take a chance. He stepped out toward the shed, turning in his stride, and as he did so he heard a cold, flat voice. "Where you goin', hombre?"

Ross turned. A broad-shouldered man had turned the corner of the mill and stood with leveled rifle, the muzzle two feet from Ross' shrinking gut.

"March," said the man.

Ross raised his hands, glancing once more at the mill. He knew well enough what would happen to him. They'd want no witnesses.

"Got a visitor, Cassidy!" said Ross' escort.

Cassidy turned as Ross approached. He grinned coldly. "Well, well," he said. "Lookit, Ben. We got company."

The look in Ben's eyes was like a blow across the face. "I thought he left the county," he said in a low voice. "Broke my heart it did. I ain't forgot Santo Tomas."

"You alone?" said Cassidy.

Ross nodded. Cassidy picked Ross' Colt from its holster and looked at it. "Junk," he said. "I wouldn't poke a fire with this." He tossed it into the stream.

"Where's your hoss?" said Slim.

Ross jerked his head. "Back in the woods," he said.

"We can get it later," said Cassidy. "Sid, you ready with that powder?"

The man nodded. "I can place it here," he said, thrusting a hand into a gap between the masonry, just above the level of the water.

"What about the explosion?" said another man.

Cassidy spat into the stream. "The wind is blowing toward us," he said. "There's two ridges between us and the ranch buildings. Besides, they'll likely think it was thunder. It's been thunderin' off and on all this morning."

"What about him?" said Sid. He looked at Ross.

"Yeh," repeated Ben. "What *about* him?"

"I was pullin' out," said Ross quickly. He wet his dry lips. "Look, fellas, I ain't in on this war. I was headin' north out of this country."

"You was?" said Slim. He raised his eyebrows. "And here we thought you was nice and cosy with Fitz. What'd you do? Make a pass at his sister or steal some of his cows?"

"Like you stole from the Box HN," said Ben.

Ross knew his death sentence had been passed, although none of them had said so.

Sid looked up. "Go get some more powder cans," he said. "We might as well make a good job out'a this."

The front door of the mill swung open and Sean Fitzgerald appeared. He walked toward the Box HN men. "What are you doing here on my property?" he said.

"He wants to know what we're doin' here," said Ben.

Cassidy looked sideways. "This makes a mess out'a the whole thing," he said. "Damn you, Walt! I told you to check that damned mill!"

Fitzgerald looked down at the powder can and then at the man who was bringing two more from the horses. His face went white. "You've gone quite far enough," he said. "I'll have you brought up on charges for this!"

Cassidy spat at the rancher's feet. "We ain't done nothin'," he said.

Slim shoved back his hat. "This makes it awkward," he said.

"It's our word against his," said Ben.

Ross felt a little better. They would have killed him, for he was a nobody, a drifter who could vanish and be forgotten in a short time, but to kill Sean Fitzgerald would be quite another matter. This wasn't the kind of war Hardy Newcomb wanted, perhaps not out of any softness on his part, but rather because it was not good business.

The mill door banged open and Buck Ellwood appeared, his overcoat cape thrown back and an old Spencer repeating carbine in his left hand. "Get away from that dam!" he commanded.

Cassidy stared at him. "Christ," he said. "How many more of 'em is in that damned mill!"

"It's that Bible-reading Yankee," said Ben Miller.

Sid looked up at Cassidy and then down at the powder. "Dammit," he growled. "You want me to place this stuff or not? I'm gettin' nervous with all this fight talk goin' on."

"Put it where you want it," said Cassidy. "We got orders to blow the dam, didn't we?"

"You'll face charges," warned Fitzgerald.

Cassidy hesitated.

"Don't be afraid of that one-armed bastard," said Ben. "We can take care of him."

Sid placed the first of the powder cans in the cavity. The Spencer cracked flatly and a softnosed .56/56 slug caught Sid squarely in the head. He pitched sideways into the rushing stream without a sound.

The shot triggered swift action. The man with the horses grabbed for a scabbarded rifle on one of the saddles. Ross dropped flat on the ground. Buck Ellwood flung the Spencer upward, twisting it sideways, opening the lever, then banged his cheek against the stock to close it, all in a matter of seconds, like a juggler on a stage. He leveled and fired just as Walt, the man who had been guarding Ross, fired his rifle. Ellwood jerked spasmodically. Walt fell sideways, rolled over twice and lay still. Ross grabbed for the rifle but Ben stomped on Ross' hand and kicked the side of his head as he drew his Colt with lightning speed and fired. Ellwood slammed back against the mill wall and reloaded.

Slim, who was guarding Fitzgerald, raised his Colt, but Ellwood ran forward and fired, staggering the tall man, then reloaded and fired again just as Ben drove two more slugs into the one-armed man. Ellwood reloaded even as he fell. He fired at the man who had been guarding the horse, just as the man fired at him. The Box HN hand smashed back against the nearest horse and went down on his knees, dropping his smoking rifle.

Ross rolled free of Ben and ran for the trees. A slug ripped through his left coat sleeve and another tore the heel from his left boot. He staggered sideways, saving his life, for Cassidy slammed two rounds just where Ross had been standing. Ross whirled and plunged toward the river fork. He dived cleanly, half obscured by the swirling gunsmoke, and gasped as he hit the cold water. He went down deep, then fought upward, striking his left hand against the cruel masonry of the dam. The water picked him up and dropped him over the dam into the roiling current below and he missed the iron-shod blades of the mill wheel by inches.

He looked up as the current swirled him toward the far side of the river. A bullet spat water into his face. The last thing he saw was Ben Miller firing at Sean Fitzgerald who stood there with his hands up, and the slug smashing full into the rancher's pale face.

Ross went around a bend, fighting to keep his head out of the water, his boots and soaked clothing trying to drag him down. He clawed at a tree trunk that thrust itself into the water, missed it, went down deeply, then was flung halfway over another log. He gripped the slippery trunk and pulled himself ashore. He dropped in the thick mud of the bank, choking and gasping.

The rain slashed down suddenly, veiling the woods. A cold wind swept across the fork and shook the trees. There seemed to be more than just the coldness of the fall in the wind; it felt as though it had the coldness of death.

Ross pulled himself to his feet. He staggered through the woods, stopping every now and then to listen, but he heard nothing. He reached a water-logged trail and then heard several more shots. He waited awhile, then padded through the dripping woods with squelching boots. He peered across the fork toward the rain-soaked mill. There was no sign of life. The horses were gone and so were the Box HN men, the living and the dead.

Ross waded across the shaking bridge and walked through the streaming rain toward the mill. Buck Ellwood lay face downward in the mud, still holding the repeater with which he had done such execution. Ross picked it up and levered the next round into the rifle. It was the last round of the seven carried in the magazine. Six bright brass hulls lay scattered about the dead millman.

Sean Fitzgerald lay crumpled against the stone foundation of the mill, huddled closely against it as though he had sought protection. Ross limped over to him. His gut roiled as he saw the back of the skull, smashed by a slug. The gray tweed coat back was black with blood. Ross rolled the rancher over on his back. His left arm flung outward as though in a gesture of asking for mercy. It had been smashed at the elbow. The face was gone. More than one softnosed .44/40 at close range had obliterated the man's features.

Ross turned away. The rain sluiced down, pattering on the mill, stippling the gray surface of the rushing stream, and soaking into the clothing of the two dead men. Ross looked at the mill. It was unharmed. The wheel still whirled at high speed, smoothly and efficiently, perfectly adjusted, the last handiwork of Buck Ellwood, who had loved the mill more than his own life.

CHAPTER THIRTEEN

ONCE AGAIN a weary, limping man approached the ranch buildings on the Rio Dulces, this time leading two horses instead of one, and with two dead men instead of one. The sky was dark, almost like dusk, with rain slanting down from the lowering clouds. The roaring of the Rio Dulces filled the valley with low thunder.

Ross Starkey stopped within eyeshot of the big casa. She would be there in the great house, unaware of the gruesome burden Ross was bringing back from the mill.

Mac McArthur walked hurriedly from the barn, water streaming from his slicker. He stopped and looked at Ross, pushing back his slicker to get at his Colt. "That you, Starkey?" he called out.

Ross nodded. "Where is Miss Fitzgerald?" he called.

"In the casa with Tascosa. I saw her an hour ago. What's up?"

"Get another man," said Ross.

"Greener is here. I'll get him." Mac looked back over his shoulder as he walked to the bunkhouse.

The rain pattered steadily on the canvas-wrapped bodies. Ross mechanically rolled a cigarette and lighted it. He fanned out the match and blew a puff of smoke, watching the rain beat it downward.

Mac and Greener hurried through the rain toward Ross. "Who are they, Starkey?" said Greener.

Ross looked toward the house. "Keep your voice low," he warned. "It's Mister Fitzgerald and Buck Ellwood."

"Jesus God!" said Mac. "Wait until Tascosa hears this! Who done it, Ross?"

"Never mind. Help me get them under cover."

"The shed behind the bunkhouse will do," said Greener.

They led the horses behind the bunkhouse and unloaded the stiffened bodies. Greener began to unwrap Fitzgerald's body.

"Let be!" said Ross. "You don't want to look at it."

"Is it that bad?" said Mac.

Ross nodded. He blew smoke through his nose. He seemed far away.

"You all right, Starkey?" asked Greener.

"Yeh," said Ross.

"Who's goin' to tell her?" said Mac. He jerked his head toward the casa.

"A good question," said Ross.

"It'll have to be you," said Greener nervously. "I don't want to be around the Kid when he hears about it."

Ross flipped his cigarette out into the rain. "He don't matter," he said quietly. He walked out into the rain, slicker flapping wide open.

"He looks like he seen a ghost," said Greener.

McArthur looked at the two bodies. "Likely he seen worse."

Ross walked toward the big house. The smoke from the chimney beat downward, carrying the bittersweet odor of burning firewood. Winter was on the way. He knocked on the side door. Minutes passed before he heard movement inside the house. The door swung open and Tascosa stood there. "You," he said coldly.

"Where is she?" said Ross.

"I'll tell her what you want," said the Kid.

"You takin' over now?" said Ross.

"Never mind."

"Who is it?" called Maureen.

Ross felt, rather than saw her, and when he did see her, she was more lovely than ever.

"You're soaked to the skin, Ross," she said. "Where is my brother?"

The words stuck in his throat.

"Ross?" she said.

Tascosa narrowed his eyes. "Answer the lady," he snapped.

She came closer to Ross. "What's wrong, Ross? You look so strange."

He passed a hand across his mouth. "It couldn't be helped," he blurted out.

"Is he hurt? Where is he?" she almost screamed.

Tascosa opened, then closed his mouth. He knew.

"He's dead, isn't he?" she said.

Tascosa pushed past Ross. He walked with stiff-legged strides toward the bunkhouse. Maureen tried to follow him but Ross held her back. "No," he husked. "Not yet, anyways."

She pressed her head against his wet chest and sobbed softly.

Boots squelched in the mud. Ross turned. Tascosa was walking swiftly toward the house. "Who done it?" he called out.

Ross turned. "Take it easy," he said.

"I asked you a question! I want an answer, by God!"

"Wait," said Ross. "You can't settle this thing now. You never could. It was wrong from the start. It's out of your hands now."

"Who done it?" grated Tascosa.

Ross stared at him. The killing blood was up. "Let me go and tell Hurley," he said. "He can't cover this thing up. He doesn't dare. He'll have to do something about it."

"Who done it?" said Tascosa.

Ross wet his dry lips. The Kid would find out anyway. Maybe the thought of facing those bloody-handed Box HN hardcases would slow him down long enough for Ross to get to the law. "There were six of them," he said slowly. "Box HN men. Art Cassidy, Ben Miller, Slim Bellew, a man named Sid, another named Walt, and some other hombre whose name I don't know."

"Where are they now?"

"Sid, Walt and the other man are all dead, as far as I know. Slim Bellew was wounded. As far as I know Cassidy and Miller were untouched. They all took off."

"Who killed the three?"

"Buck Ellwood."

"Fitz never carried a gun. Where were you all this time?"

Ross shrugged. "I wasn't in any position to do anything about it but save my own life."

"That figures!" jeered Tascosa.

Ross was utterly sick of the whole business. The only thing that was of any importance to him now was the young woman who clung to him. He knew now she would always be the only thing that would ever matter to him, no matter what she thought of him.

Tascosa turned on a heel and strode toward the stables.

"Don't go, Tascosa!" cried Maureen. "They'll kill you too!"

He paid no attention to her. In a few moments he was outside of the stable leading his gray. He swung up into the saddle with a smash of leather and spurred the gray toward the gate. In a moment the rain and the swaying trees hid him from sight.

"There goes death on a gray horse," said Greener.

"It's not the way," said Ross. He helped Maureen toward the house. "It's better that you do not see your brother, Maureen."

"You'll stay with me?" she half asked and half pleaded.

He wanted to. God, how he wanted to stay with her! "I'll have to go to Las Piedras," he said. "I'll have to tell Hurley."

"They'll kill you too!"

He opened the door and helped her inside. "I'll have to chance that," he said. He closed the door and they stood in the dimness of the hallway, close together. Her body shook with sobs. She raised her tear-stained face to his. There was nothing he could say, and precious little he could do. He cupped her wet face in his lean, hard hands and gently kissed her. "Wait for me," he said. Then he was gone.

He helped himself to fresh clothing in the bunkhouse and took a six-gun from a spare holster, checking the loads. He helped himself to a bottle of *aguardiente* and then went to get his claybank. He mounted and rode off in the rain, as Tascosa had done. No matter how hard he tried he did not seem to be able to shake the mud of Verde County from his boots. He was doomed to run out the string; to play to the last turn of a card.

The rain died out as he left the valley. The road was heavy with mud and the ditches were brim-full. A cold wind swept from the east and moved the heavy, lowering clouds toward the mountains, hiding their peaks in the thick, gray wool. It grew lighter for a time, but as Ross rode the adobe-lined road just outside of Las Piedras, it grew dark again, although the rain did not start up again.

No one bothered with the lone horseman who rode into the muddy *placita*, hat pulled low and cigarette pasted in a corner of his thin mouth. He dismounted stiffly in front of the sheriff's office. Yellow lamplight shone in the store windows, reflected in the many puddles. A heavily laden ranch wagon ground through the ruts, the heavy hoofs of the horses splashing mud and water high into the damp air.

Ross unbuttoned his slicker and eased the Colt in his holster. Fat lot of good six rounds would do him in Las Piedras if the Newcomb corrida come looking for him. He opened the door of the sheriff's office and walked in. Dan Hurley looked up from his desk and his plump face went pale. "I thought you left Verde County," he said.

Ross shook his head. "There's been a double killing on the 'Shamrock,'" he said quietly.

"Who was killed?"

"Sean Fitzgerald and Buck Ellwood."

Hurley narrowed his eyes and stood up. "Who did it?"

"Box HN men," said Ross.

"Do you know who they were?"

Ross nodded. "Art Cassidy, Slim Bellew, Ben Miller, and some others was mixed up in it too. Man by the name of Sid, another by the name of Walt. I don't know who the other one was. As far as I know, Walt, Sid and the other man are dead. I think Slim was wounded."

"Who killed them?"

"Buck Ellwood."

Hurley stared in disbelief. "Him? I don't believe it! It must have been an ambush! You saw all this? You must have been mixed up in it."

Ross began to roll a cigarette. "I'm the only living witness." He grinned crookedly. "You'd better watch me well, sheriff, because those three Box HN waddies won't want me to talk."

Hurley wiped the cold sweat from his round face. "Wait until Newcomb hears this. Gawdamighty! He didn't want anything like this. No! Never in a thousand years."

"Well, he's got it," said Ross dryly. "God, how he's got it!" He lighted the cigarette. "Another thing: the Tascosa Kid knows about the killings. He's out lookin' for Cassidy, Bellew and Miller right now. Maybe here."

Hurley jammed on his hat. He jerked his slicker from a hook. "I'll have to get Newcomb," he said.

Ross stood in the way. "Why?" he said. "This is your job. You can't stay in office forever always takin' orders from him.

This is bigger than Hardy Newcomb now, Hurley. You either settle this on your own, or you won't be wearing that star long, and maybe you'll end up in the Territorial Prison."

"They've got nothing on me," blustered the lawman.

"No?" said Ross quietly.

Hurley read something in Ross' eyes that he did not like. This battered, slow-spoken drifter knew something; something that boded no good for Dan Hurley. "You'd better come with me," he said. "You won't be bothered as long as you're with me."

"Can I count on that?"

There was a different air about the officer. "Yes," he said decisively. "You're right, Starkey. This *is* my job, and by God, I'm going to handle it myself!"

"*Bueno,*" said Ross dryly.

They walked out into the muddy street. "Newcomb is at the hotel," said the sheriff. "I'd better warn him anyway. Don't worry, Starkey. I'll see to it that no trouble starts here."

A tall man rounded the corner, running awkwardly through the mud, looking back over his shoulder, his right arm in a sling. "No!" he yelled. He saw Hurley. "For Christ's sake, Hurley! Help me! It's the Kid! He's goin' to kill me!" It was Slim Bellew.

The Kid walked swiftly around the corner, slickerless, his lean hands hanging by his sides, the right fingertips brushing the low-slung, tied-down holster.

"Stand back!" yelled Hurley.

Ross slammed a shoulder against Hurley, driving him back just as Tascosa drew and fired. Slim spun about and staggered sideways. Two more slugs rapped into him and he was flung backward by the impact of the soft, heavy slugs. He splashed into the mud.

Boots thudded on a wet boardwalk and spurs chimed as a broad-shouldered man ran toward Tascosa. "He got Slim, Ben!" he yelled.

"Stay out of this, Cassidy!" yelled Hurley.

Cassidy drew and fired, and Tascosa's shot was like an echo. Cassidy went down on his knees. He looked at the Kid. "No more," he pleaded, then he fell face forward in the mud.

Ben Miller came from between two buildings. He looked at the two Box HN men in the street and then at Tascosa. He walked toward him. Doors burst open up and down the street. Boots thudded on boardwalks or squelched in the pasty whitish mud. Ben Miller stepped over the sprawled body of Slim. "You ain't dealin' with them two now," he said.

Tascosa slid his smoking gun into its sheath. "No?" he said softly. "Who am I dealin' with?"

"Ben Miller!" rasped the Box HN man. He slapped his hand down for a draw. Tascosa's slug hit the short man in the chest. He turned about and then fired again, driving forward, firing his Colt. Tascosa fired his last round. Ben jerked with the impact. He fired once more, went down on his knees and emptied his gun into the mud, game to the last.

Tascosa ran forward and picked up Cassidy's muddy six-gun. "Stand back!" he cried out.

Hurley's face was fish-belly white. "Wait, Kid," he said. "Throw down that gun! This is the law talking!"

"Law, shit," said the Kid coldly. "Where's Newcomb?"

"Put down that gun," said Hurley. He walked forward. Ten feet from the Kid he dropped his outstretched hand to his side and in so doing, he signed his death sentence. Tascosa fired from hip level. Hurley fell sideways and then doubled over.

Ross looked at the Kid's face through the smoke. It didn't seem real, as though it was made of two halves that didn't quite fit together; almost as though one side was moving up while the other was moving down, and the eyes did not blink. "Where's Newcomb?" said the Kid in a strange voice.

"You'd better beat it, Kid!" yelled a man from the crowd.

The Kid still stared at Ross, Colt at hip level, a thin wisp of smoke rising from the hot muzzle, and if Ross Starkey had ever looked at death, he was looking at it now.

Slowly, ever so slowly, the Kid backed away, swinging the Colt from side to side, until he reached the corner, and then he darted around it.

"Go get him!" yelled Hardy Newcomb from the back of the crowd as he began to force his way through.

"Go get him yourself, Newcomb!" yelled someone. "You started all this!"

"Who said that?" roared the rancher.

Ross leaned against an awning post. He slowly began to fashion a cigarette. He heard the thudding of hoofs in a side street and it seemed far, far away.

Newcomb looked at Ross. "What did you have to do with this, Starkey?" he demanded.

Ross looked at him as he lighted the cigarette. "Nothing," he said quietly. "But I aim to have something to do about it."

"Such as?"

Ross blew a smoke ring. "Wait and see," he said. He walked to his horse and untethered it.

Newcomb came up behind him. "Why did he come to Las Piedras?" he said.

Ross turned. "Your boys killed Fitzgerald and Buck Ellwood at the mill," he said.

"You're lying!"

Ross looked past the tough old boot into the cold faces of half a dozen Newcomb hardcases. "No, I ain't," he said. "I come into town to tell Hurley. For once Hurley was goin' to handle the law without your advice."

"You can't talk to me like that!" snapped Newcomb.

"Oh, yes I can," said Ross. "I'm doin' just that. The Kid must'a gone loco. He come lookin' for them three, and you too. Lucky you was out of sight. Dan Hurley's luck run out."

Newcomb narrowed his hard eyes. A look of respect came into them. "My men killed Fitzgerald and Ellwood?" he asked.

Ross nodded.

"I had nothing to do with it."

"You sent them to blow the mill dam, didn't you?"

Newcomb hesitated. He looked back at the silent crowd.

"You don't have to say anything," said Ross.

"There was to be no shooting!"

"No? Well, damn you, you started that avalanche, and you couldn't stop it. By God, Newcomb, you're goin' to reap the storm that's goin' to hit this damned bloody county!" Ross swung up on the claybank and rode toward the street that led to the Rio Dulces Road.

"Where are you goin'?" called out Newcomb.

Ross turned in the saddle. "To deliver a letter," he said. He turned and rode on. The rain began to fall steadily, pocking the churned mud, streaming from the roof eaves, slowly washing the blood from the faces of the stiffening dead.

CHAPTER FOURTEEN

Ross Starkey tethered his horse outside of his brother's house in Santa Fe. It had been a fine fall day on the ride up from Galisteo, but with the coming of the swift dusk had come a cold wind that swept down from the Sangre de Cristos, blowing dust and fallen leaves through the narrow, winding streets, rattling and banging the shutters, moaning across the flat-topped roofs of the ancient city.

He walked to the door and dropped the heavy knocker several times. It had been a long and lonely ride up from Las Piedras, with plenty of time for thought.

"Quién es?" called a feminine voice from beyond the door.

"It is Señor Ross Starkey," he said in Spanish, "brother to Señor Starkey."

"Wait one moment," she said.

In a little while chains rattled, and the door swung open. Lloyd Starkey stood there in the yellow lamplight, a warm smile on his face. His hair and mustache had grayed and there were more lines on his face, but his eyes were still young. "The Prodigal Son," said Lloyd. "I was just thinking about you today."

"Nice thoughts?" said Ross.

"Why not?"

Ross grinned. "I'm relieved," he said.

"Come on in!"

Ross jerked his head. "My horse is out there."

"Manuel will get him," said Lloyd. He led the way into the big casa.

Ross looked about as they crossed a wide patio, complete with shade trees and a fountain. Lloyd was doing well for himself.

Lloyd looked back. "The house comes with the job," he said.

"Such as?"

Lloyd opened a door and ushered Ross into a sitting room. "Legal aide to the new governor," he said.

"You're getting up in the world."

"I'm doing the best I can. Sit down. Warm yourself. Have you eaten?"

"Not since leaving Galisteo this morning."

"Galisteo? You've come a long way from the Rio Dulces."

Ross listened to his brother give orders to his woman servant. He looked about the low-ceilinged room. The firelight and lamplight glistened from the heavy, waxed furniture and the paintings on the walls.

Lloyd walked to a sideboard. "Wine before dining?" he said.

"Any time," said Ross. "Before, during and after."

"You haven't changed much."

"How did you know I came from the Rio Dulces?"

Lloyd placed the wine glass on the table beside Ross and then sat down opposite him, studying him with appraising gray eyes. "We have been interested in Verde County for quite some time," he said. He sipped at his wine. "We knew when you arrived there. We knew about your fight in Santo Tomas. We knew about the horrible killing of Francisco Ochoa. We've been investigating this so-called 'Verde County war', and we don't like it. The new governor has given me carte blanche to clean it up in any way I see fit."

Ross nodded. He felt inside his shabby coat and withdrew the thick, sealed envelope Maureen Fitzgerald had given him. "Do you know the latest from Verde County?"

"We had information some days ago."

"About the latest killings?"

Lloyd narrowed his eyes. "The last we had heard was about the man named Ochoa."

Ross emptied his glass. "Drink up," he said. "Refill the glasses. You're going to need it."

Lloyd listened silently while Ross filled in the bloody details he had witnessed during the killings at the mill and in the muddy *placita* of Las Piedras. The woman came in silently and placed the food on the table and refilled the wineglasses. The fire crackled as she placed fresh wood on it and then she left as silently as she had come, and all the time Ross spoke in a low voice, missing no details.

Lloyd emptied his glass and stood up. He paced back and forth while Ross ate, a cigar clenched between his teeth, leaving a trail of bluish smoke behind him as he read the long letter written by Sean Fitzgerald. He finished it as Ross finished his meal. Ross refilled his wineglass, eased off his boots and lighted a cigar. He felt somewhat pleased with himself. He had escaped the blood bath of Verde County.

Lloyd stood by the fire, looking into the flickering flames. "Who will succeed Dan Hurley as sheriff?" he asked.

Ross shrugged. "He's got a deputy. Fella by the name of Grant Orris, or something like that. Not much more than a process server, they say. Anyway, Hardy Newcomb will have his say-so on who takes over."

"Not anymore," said Lloyd firmly.

"Do you know him?"

"We've met," said Lloyd grimly. "When the Territorial Legislation was in session last year. He bulled through half a dozen bills of his own, without ever opening his mouth in the Legislature."

"That's him," said Ross dryly.

"The new governor has written to him. Hardy Newcomb may have met his match in the governor. The governor's orders are to clean up Verde County."

"Good luck," said Ross. He blew a cloud of smoke toward the nearest lamp and watched the smoke swirl upward.

"This Tascosa Kid—he must have left the county by now?"

"*Quién sabe?*"

Lloyd nodded. "I'll know in a few days. Meanwhile I'll talk to the governor. What are your plans?"

Ross rubbed his bristly jaw. He looked up at his brother. "I need something from you to work them out."

"Such as?" Lloyd studied his younger brother. "By God, there's something different about you! Maybe you want to study law? You can clerk for me. You're sharp enough to catch on. A little hard work and a burning of the midnight oil, and you can pass the bar examination. I can use a partner."

Ross shook his head. "It's not that, Lloyd. Thanks anyway."

Lloyd relighted his cigar. "It's the old ranch, isn't it?"

"You've hit on it."

"It's yours. You can pay off my share when you get around to it." Lloyd fanned out the match. He tilted his head to one side. "There's something else, isn't there?"

Ross grinned. "I never could lie to you."

Lloyd stared at him. "A woman? By God, I mean a *lady*? With *you*?"

Ross looked into the fireplace. "I know it's hard to believe," he said awkwardly.

"Who is she, Ross?"

Ross looked up. "Maureen Fitzgerald," he said.

Lloyd worked his cigar over to the other side of his mouth. "You always were full of surprises. Have you asked her yet? I've heard she is a beauty."

Ross blew a smoke ring. "No, to your question. Yes, to your statement. Of course, I ain't sure she'd marry an old warhorse like me, but I aim to ask her as soon as I get back there."

Lloyd grinned. "Old warhorse? Hell, you won't be thirty for another year and a half! She couldn't find herself a better man, providing he gets some sense in his thick head and sticks to ranching on the Canadian."

"I aim to," said Ross.

Lloyd looked serious. "Is she all right, now that her brother is gone?"

Ross looked up quickly. "No man in Verde County would be loco enough to bother her," he said.

Lloyd nodded. "Not with the Tascosa Kid riding guard on her." He was startled at the look on Ross' lean face. "Did I say something wrong?"

Ross flipped his cigarette butt into the fireplace. "No," he said. "You didn't know. The Kid and I met in Mexico some time ago. I won't say how, or why. We were amigos until a little while ago."

"What happened?"

Ross rolled a cigarette and lighted it. He looked at his brother over the flare of the match. "If I go back, he'll likely try to kill me."

"Then don't go back."

Ross stood up and walked to the fireplace. He looked into the dancing flames. "I got no choice, Lloyd," he said quietly. "I *got* to go back."

In the days that followed Ross Starkey's arrival in Santa Fe, news drifted up from Verde County that the Tascosa Kid had killed another Box HN man and had escaped into the hills. There was more; something that had an ominous ring to it. The Spanish-speaking New Mexicans of Verde County, those of the old stock, were, for the most part, deeply sympathetic to the Kid. They were hiding him, protecting him, making a hero out of him. The Robin Hood of Verde County. Of such is legend made.

Lloyd asked Ross to come with him for an interview with the new governor. There was a curious feeling of foreboding in Ross when he met the Territorial chief executive, a straight-backed, level-eyed, bearded ex-soldier of the Civil War. Ross was almost convinced during the preliminaries of conversation that Hardy Newcomb might indeed have met his match.

"The Tascosa Kid is still on the loose," said the governor as he shoved a cigar box across his desk toward the two brothers. "Still in Verde County. Still as elusive as a ghost. He can't be caught by ordinary means. The Box HN men won't go into the hills after him. The other ranchers want no part of him, and he doesn't bother them anyway. The Spanish-speaking New Mexicans look up to him as a sort of hero. As long as they do so, he is safe from being arrested."

Ross lighted his cigar. "He's only one man," he said quietly.

Lloyd and the governor exchanged glances. Lloyd leaned toward his brother. "There isn't any law-abiding American in Verde County who doesn't want to see the Kid brought in to justice. We agree there was provocation for the Kid in the first part, but not to the bloody extent that he has taken his revenge. He has many friends. It will be difficult to capture him. *But we must get him, or the Verde County war will not end!* The governor is prepared to go easy on him if he agrees to give himself up. Perhaps a long jail sentence. Certainly not the death penalty."

Ross blew a smoke ring. "A jail sentence would be worse than the death penalty for the Kid," he said quietly. "You don't know him like I do."

There was a moment's silence. The governor suddenly became deeply interested in the end of his cigar. "Exactly," he said. "Apparently there isn't *anyone* who knows him as well as you do."

Ross slowly took his cigar from his mouth. He looked at his brother. "What's on your mind, Lloyd? You didn't bring me here for a social visit with the governor."

Lloyd stood up and paced back and forth. "The governor is prepared to pardon the Kid, with the stipulation that he must serve a term in the Territorial Prison. The problem we have is in contacting the Kid. Someone whom the Kid trusts will have to find him and deliver the governor's message."

Ross got the idea. "Like me," he said dryly.

"I can commission you as a special officer of the Territory of New Mexico," said the governor.

"That won't cut any ice with the Kid," said Ross. "By this time he has no more use for me than he does for the Box HN men."

"Would he believe you if you offered him the governor's amnesty?" said Lloyd.

"If I was covered by a company of cavalry and a Gatling gun," said Ross. "He'll never let me get within pistol range."

"We haven't anyone else to do the job," said the governor.

Ross blew a smoke ring and watched it drift slowly toward an open window. "I ain't too popular with Hardy Newcomb down Verde County way," he said.

"I have telegraphed to him," said the governor. "I have his assurance by return wire he will not interfere with you."

"I'd rather trust a diamondback," said Ross. He looked into the governor's eyes and knew right then and there that Hardy Newcomb *had* at last met his match.

"What about it, Ross?" said Lloyd, "You have to go back there anyway. You must consider the position of Maureen Fitzgerald."

Ross quickly looked at him. "What do you mean?"

"We have information by telegraph that the Kid has taken it on himself to 'protect' her, with the result that she lives virtually alone on the Rio Dulces ranch. Any trespassers, innocent or not, have to deal with the Kid. It's said she is deathly afraid of him. It's also said he won't harm her. But she's like a princess guarded by a two-headed ogre or a ferocious dragon."

"Two-gun," the governor said.

Ross slowly snubbed out the cigar. "Write out the commission," he said quietly. "I always knew I'd have to face the Kid again some day."

The governor quickly opened a drawer and withdrew a legal-looking paper, stamped with the Territorial seal. He signed it swiftly. "Stand up and raise your right hand," he said.

Ross grinned wryly. "Well, I'll be double-damned," he said.

Later, with the governor's final instructions still ringing in his ears, Ross walked across the plaza toward La Fonda with his brother. "This might easily be *my* death sentence," said Ross. He looked at his brother. "But, like I said back there, I always knew I'd have to face the Kid again some day. *One way or another I'll have to face him.* My life seems bound up with that of the Kid—win, lose or draw."

"Do you think you can get him?"

Ross stopped in mid-stride. "What do you mean by that?"

Lloyd shrugged. "You don't *have* to bring him in alive," he said. "That commission covers you all the way, Ross. *All* the way . . ."

"Like a hunting license, eh?"

"Exactly."

Ross began to fashion a smoke. He looked up at the blue, cloud-dotted sky and inhaled the fresh, winey air. "Suddenly I feel cold all over," he said.

"You're doing a service to the Territory, Ross. To Maureen Fitzgerald. To all men."

Ross lighted the cigarette. "It ain't that easy," he said. "I've hunted men and I've been hunted by men. This feels different somehow. I ain't sure that I'm going to like it at all."

"You won't do it then?"

There was a pause, then Ross looked directly into his brother's eyes, and Lloyd Starkey knew then and there he was no longer looking at a "kid" brother, but rather at a fully grown man, skilled with weapons, equally dangerous on either side of the law. "I didn't say that," said Ross at last.

"Come on. I owe you one drink at least."

Ross shook his head. "The day is young. The road is long. I'd better be on my way."

Lloyd thrust out his hand. "The ranch will be waiting for you and your bride," he said heartily.

Ross nodded. "Yes," he said in a faraway voice. He turned on a heel and walked away, followed by the thoughtful eyes of his older brother.

In an hour he was on the Galisteo Road, south of Santa Fe, riding steadily toward Verde County and his destiny, as well as that of the Tascosa Kid.

CHAPTER FIFTEEN

THE WIND HAD SHIFTED during the long sunny afternoon, and as Ross Starkey threaded a narrow, high-walled pass west of the Rio Dulces, he heard the faint, intermittent ringing of a bell from the high country to his left. He shifted in his saddle and looked up at the broken-toothed peaks, still tipped with the bright light of the sinking sun. The bell had stopped, or had he heard a bell at all? No one lived up there, or at least no one had lived up there to his knowledge. It was a trick of the wind, or perhaps of his imagination.

The claybank's hoofs struck chiming music from the rocky bed of the pass and echoed from the high walls. The wind moaned softly from the east. He cleared the mouth of the pass and drew rein to look down upon the vast panorama of the Rio Dulces country. He could see the oases made by men on the open land. Where there was water, there would be a house, and around the house would rise the waving greenery that protected it from the hot suns of the summer and the cold, thin winter air of those altitudes. Rising above the waving trees were thin wraiths of wispy, bluish smoke. Far across the rolling stretches of the lower ground he could see dust rising beyond a ridge. That would likely be on the road to Las Piedras.

He looked to the south, expecting to see the rooftop of the great casa of the "Shamrock" spread, but couldn't distinguish it at that distance. No smoke arose from it. He touched the tired claybank with his heels and rode down the twisting road, and as he did so he heard again the faint, insistent ringing of a bell. He turned again in his saddle and looked up at the higher country. No one lived up there, or at least there would be no church or chapel up there. He had heard vague stories of a lost village in this country, but the Mexes were always thinking up such stories. It was a trick of the wind, and yet he was sure he had heard something.

The sun was gone when he reached the Rio Dulces Valley. It grew colder after the warm day. He buttoned up his coat and rolled a cigarette. The wind moaned along the darkened valley. He looked toward the higher ground west of the river, expecting to see the lights of the Fitzgerald casa, but they were not to be seen.

He crossed the rushing river on the old bridge and looked toward the thick motte where Tascosa had always posted a rifleman. Ross whistled sharply, three times and then twice, but he heard nothing but the faint echoing of the signal. Maybe it had been changed by the "Shamrock" corrida.

He rode gingerly toward the motte, but there was no one there. The gate creaked loudly as he opened it, but the noise brought no response, no sharp challenge from the darkness, coupled with the sound of a rifle lever being worked. No dog barked. No lights showed. He swung down from the claybank and drew his rifle from its scabbard. He ground out the cigarette beneath a boot and padded quietly toward the ranch buildings, the horse's reins looped about his left arm.

He halted between the big bunkhouse and the casa. Still no lights and no sound. He dropped the reins of the clay-bank and walked toward the bunkhouse. He tried the door and it swung open easily. Ross walked inside and snapped a match on a thumbnail. The faint, flickering light showed that the place was empty of life. The bunks were stripped. Dust rose about his feet as he walked from one end of the echoing building to the other. The foreman's room was empty. A broken rye bottle lay in a corner.

Ross walked outside and checked the cookhouse. The stove had long been cold and the mess table in the dining room was thick with dust and the tiny tracks of mice.

He walked outside and looked toward the great casa. Not a light showed. He walked toward it, looking back toward the corrals. They too were empty. The place was like a ghost ranch. He called out as he reached the house but there was no answer. He tried two doors and found them locked. A weak window lock allowed him to enter the big kitchen. He rooted about and found a bull's-eye lantern which he lighted.

In twenty minutes he had covered the house from kitchen up to the topmost rooms, and not a sign of life did he find, except a bright-eyed mouse that vanished beneath a bed as he entered one of the dusty rooms. No one had been in the casa for weeks, from the evidence.

He walked downstairs and into the dark study. He lighted a lamp and looked about. The place was undisturbed. He helped himself to a stiff drink from the sideboard and sat down in a chair. Where were Maureen Fitzgerald and her employees? The curious thing about the whole mystery was that the place was undisturbed. There had been no vandalism and no looting. News traveled fast in that country and if some of the people had learned that the great rancho and its hacienda on the Rio Dulces had been deserted, it would have been stripped of anything of value in a few days.

Ross poked about and found a half-empty box of cigars. He bit the end off one and lighted it. It was dry, but satisfying. Maybe she had left the country and gone back to her people in Ireland, or had moved into one of the towns nearby. There was one thing that stuck in his mind. Something his brother Lloyd had said. "The Kid has taken it on himself to 'protect' her, with the result that she lives virtually alone on the Rio Dulces ranch. Any trespassers, innocent or not, have to deal with the Kid. It's said that she's deathly afraid of him. Oh, he won't harm her. Not the way one might think. But it's like she's living in isolation, like a princess guarded by a ferocious dragon or a two-headed ogre."

Ross looked about at the gathering dust. The fireplace had long been cold. Suddenly he had an eerie feeling that he was being watched. He looked quickly about, then laughed. The place was getting on his nerves. He slid a full bottle into each pocket and put out the lamp. He had no desire to stay the night anywhere near the place, and he had to know where Maureen was, and then try to get a line on Tascosa.

He walked through the echoing hall and into the kitchen. He blew out the bull's-eye lamp and placed it on the table. He looked back along the dark hallway, shivered again, then walked outside into the faint moonlight. The whole damned place gave him the creeps. He felt for one of the bottles, pulled out the cork and raised it to his lips. Something flashed amidst the shrubbery beyond the walled yard and a gun crack followed at the instant the rye bottle was shattered at Ross' lips, spraying his face with broken glass and good rye. Half blinded, he threw the bottle neck aside and dropped flat on the flags, feeling for his Colt.

It was very quiet after the echo of the shot died away. Ross slowly wiped the blood and whiskey from his burning face.

"What are you doing here, Starkey?" said the cold voice from the shrubbery.

"Kid?" said Ross.

There was no answer, nothing but the faint sound of the shrubbery moving in the night wind. Ross shifted and the broken glass tinkled beneath him. He eased out his Colt.

The voice came from the right beyond the wall. "I can see every move you make, Starkey," said the Kid.

Ross felt cold sweat break out on his body. The bastard moved like a ghost!

"It's a good thing for you I recognized you," said the Kid.

"Why?" said Ross dryly. "We didn't part amigos."

"I haven't forgotten El Corralitos. You saved my life there. I don't forget things like that."

Ross wiped away a sticky trickle of blood from his cheek. "Where is Miss Maureen?" he asked.

"What's it to you?"

"I've got a message for her."

"You can give it to me."

"Where is she?"

There was a long pause and when the Kid spoke again it was from a different spot, and yet Ross hadn't seen or heard a thing. Only an Apache could move like that. "Give me the message," said the Kid.

"I have to deliver it personally."

"Who is it from?"

Ross took a long chance. "The governor," he said.

The Kid laughed.

"You think I'm lying?" said Ross.

"You're too stupid to lie well."

"*Gracias.*"

"I thought you went back to see Consuelo Orcutt," said the Kid. "Where have you been all this time?"

Ross spat. "Listen," he said. "The governor is out to get you, one way or another, Kid. I was sent down here to talk with you. I didn't think it would be this easy to find you."

"I found you," said the Kid. "Looting."

"For God's sake listen to me! The governor has had enough of this damned Verde County feud! He knows everything that is happening down here. My brother is his legal aide. Between the two of them they commissioned me to talk with you."

"They must be hard up for help."

"That's neither here nor there!"

"What's the deal?" said the Kid.

"You'll get a pardon."

"What's the price?"

Ross hesitated.

"There *is* a price, isn't there?" said the Kid. His voice came from another place, almost as though he was throwing it where he willed. An eerie feeling came over Ross. If he could only see the Kid!

"Well?" said the Kid.

"A prison term," said Ross at last.

The Kid laughed. "Big deal! Let 'em come and get me!"

"They will," said Ross. "The whole county is against you and the governor means to get you. If you don't listen to me, and take the governor's proposition, the ranchers will hunt you down. Hardy Newcomb alone can do it with his corrida."

The Kid laughed again. "Hardy Newcomb!" he jeered. "He won't ever bother Miss Maureen or me again."

Ross narrowed his eyes. He couldn't even see a thickening of the shadows where the Kid stood. "Did you kill him too?" asked Ross.

"No. Something worse for Hardy Newcomb."

"Such as?"

"Go and see. It's worth the ride to Las Piedras." The Kid laughed. "Take the other bottle with you. Compliments of the house. Hardy Newcomb could do with a drink."

Ross peered into the shadows. "Kid?" he said.

There was no answer. The wind swayed the brush.

Minutes dragged past and Ross got slowly to his feet,

half expecting another bullet. He wiped his face with his scarf and took out the second bottle. This time he got his drink. He drove the cork in with the heel of his hand and walked to the wall. The moonlight was sufficient for him to see that the shrubbery was not occupied. He dropped over the wall and looked about. There wasn't a mark on the soft earth. Not a boot print. An eerie feeling came over him again.

He walked to the claybank and sheathed his rifle. Once more he looked about. The place was thoroughly deserted.

He rode toward the bridge. The moonlight showed on the cleared area where the ranch graveyard was situated on a rise overlooking the river bottoms. Each headboard and gravestone stood out. He kneed the claybank close to the wall to look at the mounded graves. All of them were empty of flowers except the freshest grave, set off by itself on slightly higher ground. The moonlight shone on the carved headstone. It was the grave of Sean Fitzgerald, and those fall flowers had been put there that very day, perhaps that very night.

Ross crossed the bridge, the hairs prickling on the back of his neck, not daring to look back for fear of seeing a ghostly horseman on a gray horse following him through the patches of moonlight and the dark stretches of shadows.

CHAPTER SIXTEEN

THE DESK CLERK looked up as Ross Starkey opened the front door of the Las Piedras House. He frowned a little as he saw the dusty, lean-looking man, wearing a faded hat. Ross crossed the carpeted lobby, ignoring the looks of the people seated about the lobby. His spurs chimed softly until he stopped in front of the desk. "I want to see Hardy Newcomb," he said.

"*Mister* Newcomb?" said the clerk. He moved back a little as though to avoid the faint mingled aromas of sweat, trail dust, horseflesh, stale tobacco smoke and pungent rye.

"That's him," said Ross.

"Have you an appointment?"

Ross smiled faintly. "In a way," he said.

"He isn't receiving visitors tonight."

Ross looked past the clerk to the pigeonholes. One of them had a neatly lettered script above it. "Room four," said Ross. He walked toward the carpeted stairs.

"You can't just go up there like that!" cried the clerk.

Ross kept on climbing the wide staircase.

"Besides, it's not a *room*, it's a *suite*!" said the clerk.

Ross tapped on the suite door. It swung open and a professional-looking man stood there, a leather case under his arm and his hat in his hand. "Yes?" he said.

"My name is Starkey," said Ross. "Ross Starkey. I want to see Hardy Newcomb."

"I'm Doctor Daily. I don't think Mister Newcomb is receiving visitors."

"Who is it, Doc?" cried out a familiar voice.

"A man named Ross Starkey," said the doctor over his shoulder.

There was a long pause. "Let him in, Doc," said Newcomb.

"I don't want him here too long," said the doctor.

"A few minutes," said Ross. "What's the matter with the old man?"

Daily stood aside. "See for yourself," he said. He walked past Ross and closed the door behind him.

Ross took off his hat, glanced down at his holstered Colt, then walked into the sitting room. A white head showed above the back of a wing chair standing in front of a window that gave a clear view of the distant mountains to the west, dreaming under the soft light of the fall moon.

"Come around this way," said the rancher. "You're safe, Starkey."

"I wasn't worried," said Ross.

"The hell you ain't!"

Ross grinned. Whatever else was the matter with the old bastard, he still had his teeth.

He walked around the chair and looked down at the old man and a shock came through him. Just weeks ago Hardy Newcomb had been as tough-looking as an old boot, but he had aged and there was a physical weakness showing on his lined face.

The rancher waved a thin hand. "Set," he said. "I look like hell. You don't have to say it."

"I wasn't going to."

Newcomb shifted a little, wincing in sudden pain. His legs were swathed in a thick blanket from the waist down. "I heard from the governor," he said. "You took your time getting here."

"I didn't know I was supposed to report to you."

Newcomb shrugged. "It wasn't that. I wanted to warn you about the Kid. He's gone loco in my opinion." He looked down at his legs. "He made me pay a price."

"What do you mean?"

"Drygulched me when I went over to the Rio Dulces, my pride in my hand, to see what I could do for Miss Maureen. I never got beyond the bridge, Starkey. Another half an inch and the bullet would have cut my spine in half. The bullet is still in there." He wiped cold sweat from his forehead. "I'll never walk again. Damn me if I don't believe he did it on purpose."

Ross felt for the makings. "I saw him tonight, or at least heard him tonight."

"You talk in riddles."

Ross told him of his experience at the casa.

Newcomb nodded. "It's his style," he said quietly. "The Mexes are starting to call him *El Espectro*." He laughed. "Maybe it's what he always wanted."

"Where is Maureen Fitzgerald?"

Newcomb shrugged. *"Quién sabe?"* No one can get near the ranch. All the hands pulled out weeks ago. The 'Shamrock' corrida is gone. They won't be back."

"And the Box HN?"

Newcomb looked up at him. "I lost my three best men that night out in the street. I'm through with this fighting, Starkey."

Ross leaned against the wall and lighted his cigarette. "About time," he said.

"I can get you help," said the old man.

"Box HN waddies? Hell no! I'd never get near the Kid with them riding with me."

"What makes you think you can get near him any other way?"

Ross looked out toward the silvered mountains. The Kid was somewhere up there most likely. "I don't know," he said.

"I'll tell my boys to stay away from his haunts."

Ross nodded. "You know about the pardon the governor is offering?"

"Yes. Do you think he'll accept it?"

Ross shook his head.

"Neither do I. Go back to Santa Fe and forget the whole thing. As long as the local Mexes are with him, and he's in those damned hills and mountains, a battalion of Texas Rangers couldn't get to him."

"Somebody has to do it."

"Why you?"

"Who else is there?"

"Is it that young woman?"

Ross turned and looked down at him. "Yes," he said. "I love her and I think she loves me."

"You ain't too bright, Starkey. I always said that."

"Gracias," said Ross dryly.

Newcomb winced in pain. "Somebody has to get him," he said, almost as though to himself. "Maybe you're the one. By God, I wouldn't want the job! He's as slick as an Apache, as cruel as a Comanche, and deadlier with guns than any man I've ever seen or heard about. You're no match for him, Starkey. You go up in those mountains and you won't ever come out again."

Ross blew a smoke ring. "I have to go," he said.

Newcomb shrugged. "Anything you need?"

"My horse is wore out."

"Go down to the livery stable. Tell Max Gifford to give you any horse you want. Anything else? A room for the night? Money? You name it, Starkey."

Ross smiled. "I'll take the hoss and your good wishes," he said.

The rancher nodded. He twisted around to watch Ross walk to the door. *"Vaya con Dios,"* he said.

Ross did not speak. He closed the door behind him. His spurs chimed softly as he walked toward the head of the stairs.

Hardy Newcomb wiped the cold sweat from his face. He looked toward the dreaming mountains to the west. "By God," he said quietly. "He's on a high lonesome if any man ever was." He grimaced in pain. "At that, it would be worth seeing those two face each other for the final showdown!"

There was no sleep in Ross that night, tired as he was. He traded off his worn-out claybank for a blocky dun and left Las Piedras. He wanted no part of that town. He looked back as he crossed the bridge, toward the tallest building in town, the Las Piedras House, owned, of course by Hardy Newcomb. Well, it was his prison now, just as much as though there were bars on the windows and guards at the doors. Hardy Newcomb would probably never leave that hotel alive.

The moon swung upward in its course, flooding the Valley of the Rio Dulces. There was no sign of life except the lone horseman who rode steadily westward, avoiding the deserted ranch, to strike into the hills. Ross had followed this hidden trail, just once, heading the other way, guided by Tascosa after Ross' epic fight in the streets of Santo Tomas with Art Cassidy, Slim Bellew and Ben Miller. They were all dead now, and this time Ross was guided only by the sheer instinct he had for remembering any trail he had ever taken, though it might have been years past. The faculty had kept him alive more than once.

The moon was long gone when he emerged from the tor-

tuous passages and saw Santo Tomas far below him, marked
by a few faint lights and the fainter odor of burning wood.

The door of the Santo Tomas Cantina opened as Ross rode
slowly toward it. Three men staggered out and walked the
other way, laughing and talking, not seeing the horseman behind them. In a little while they were gone. Ross dismounted
and tethered the dun in the same *ramada* he had used the
last time he had graced Santo Tomas with his presence. He
rapped on the cantina door when he found it locked.

"*Quién es?*" called out Fedro. "It is late. I am closed."

"It is the Señor Starkey," said Ross.

"Go away! He is dead, they say."

Ross clinked two silver dollars together. There was a short
wait and then the bars rattled and the door swung open to
reveal Fedro holding a lantern high in his hand, peering at
Ross. "*Madre de Dios!*" he said. "It *is* you! Come in! Come
in!" He closed and barred the door behind Ross.

Ross walked to the bar and leaned wearily on it. "Any
chance for a drink?"

Fedro nodded. "First you owe me for the bottle you took
from here the day you fought those men in the street. Such a
fight! Already Pablo Diaz, our village poet, has written a
canción about it. It is very good."

Ross paid for the long-empty bottle and another was shoved
toward him. Ross filled his glass. "Will you drink with me?"
he said.

Fedro smiled, the lamplight flashing on his white teeth. "It
is a pleasure! What brings you back to Santo Tomas?"

Ross downed the good brandy. He winced in pleasure.
"I'm looking for the Tascosa Kid," he said.

Fedro stared at him. "*Madre de diablo!* Surely you jest!"

Ross reached across the bar and helped himself to a
cigar. He bit off the end and lighted it. "No," he said. "Where
is he?"

Fedro spread out his fat hands, palms upward, then
shrugged with his whole back and shoulders. "*Quién sabe?*"

"He can't just vanish into thin air, amigo."

"Perhaps he can."

Ross blew a smoke ring and eyed the cantina owner. "You
sayin' he's a ghost?"

Fedro sketchily crossed himself. "Some say he is dead.
That it is a ghost they see riding the hills. *El Espectro!*"

"What hills?"

Fedro shook his head. "Everywhere. It is said he is seen one night near here, and the next a hundred miles away. He has vanished on the trail within plain eyesight of men who are known for their honesty. He has been seen riding the streets of Santo Tomas at midnight under the full moon, and one can see right through him! There are those who have seen him at the Rancho de la Rio Dulces. None of my people will go there, Señor Starkey. It is haunted."

"Listen," said Ross patiently. "He ain't no ghost. He's alive! I talked with him this very night."

Fedro crossed himself again. "You *saw* him?"

Ross took the cigar from his mouth. "Well, not exactly."

"You see! Perhaps you heard his voice?"

Ross nodded.

"Ah! But you did not *see* him, eh?"

"No."

"You see!" said Fedro triumphantly.

Ross touched the glass wounds on his face. "These came from glass splinters from a bottle smashed by a bullet fired by the Tascosa Kid. Begod, amigo, that was no ghost bullet!"

"It is said some ghosts can do such things."

"Bull crap! So, you won't tell me where he has gone?"

"I don't know."

"The woman? Señorita Fitzgerald. Where is she?"

Fedro looked toward the door and lowered his voice. "She was here in Santo Tomas not too long ago. She rented a house from my cousin Ferdinand. One night there were no lights in that house. The next day Rafaela Perez went there to do the house cleaning. The Señorita Fitzgerald was gone. Her clothing and everything. Gone!" He shivered. "No one knows where she is."

Ross emptied his glass and refilled it. "She's likely with the Kid," he said.

"It is said that she is madly in love with him, but so it is with many of the women of Verde County. Men fear him and women love him. I am not at all sure I would want to be in his boots though."

Ross nodded. "Who lives in the mountains north of here?"

"No one."

"Someone must live up there," said Ross.

"Why are you so sure? It is true that some of my people lived there many years ago, but the Apaches wiped many of them out, and then the war was hard on them. The padres who lived up there were all killed by the Apaches. Then the people left, although no one saw them go, or knows of where they went. It is said that none of them left there alive."

Ross relighted his cigar. "I heard a bell ringing from up there," he said. He waited for Fedro's reply and then looked at him. The man was pasty-faced beneath his brown skin. "What's wrong?" added Ross.

Fedro drained his glass and refilled it. "It is the ghost bell," he said. "What time of the day was it?"

"Late afternoon. Almost dusk."

"*Por Dios!* It *was* the ghost bell."

"Bull crap! Someone had to ring it."

"It is from the old *placita* somewhere up there."

"Where is this *placita*?"

"*Quién sabe?* No one living knows. My people know those mountains are haunted and the Apaches will not go near them."

"So no one knows if there is a *placita* at all then?"

Fedro shrugged. "Now and then someone hears the bell. If they hear it once it is a first warning. If they hear it twice it is the second warning. If they hear it the third time . . ." His voice trailed off.

"Go on!" snapped Ross.

Fedro swallowed hard. "If it is heard the third time, the one who hears it is doomed. He will never come out of those mountains."

Ross laughed. "What do they call that place?"

"Puerta de Luna."

"The Door of the Moon? A loco name."

Fedro shook his head. "There is a narrow pass up there. One that cannot be seen by day, but at the time of the full moon, just about midnight, the rays of the sinking moon fall upon it long enough for one to find it, if he *wants* to find it."

"And if he does?"

Fedro refilled the glasses. "He can go *in*. He will never come out . . . *alive*."

"You been drinking too much of your own cheap booze," said Ross.

Fedro shrugged. "It is late. I have a bed for you."

Ross emptied his glass. The thought of a bed sounded good.

Fedro put out the lamp and led the way into the back of the cantina. He watched Ross sit down on the sagging cot. He grinned. "Your old amigo, the Kid, has known many women on that cot."

"Figures," said Ross.

Fedro hesitated. He wet his full lips. "You are a good man, Señor Starkey," he said hesitantly.. "If one was to find the Kid, he would do well to ride through the Door of the Moon." He hastily shut the door behind him.

CHAPTER SEVENTEEN

THE LATE AFTERNOON sun drove its hot rays against the steep western escarpment of the mountains. A heat haze, more common in summer than in the late fall, shimmered up from the heated rock and gave an unreal appearance to the jagged, fissured heights. The lowest slopes were marked by great fan-shaped playas of detritus washed down from the eroding rock high above. Above that the green belt of high timber stretched as far as the eye could see both to the north and to the south. Above that in turn was the naked rock above the timberline.

Ross Starkey sat in the hot shade of the lowest slopes. For three days he had probed the western approaches to the mountains with no results. "Puerta de Luna?" had said a young shepherd. "There is no such place!" An old, old man, whose sight had long been gone, had sat in the morning sun, facing the great rampart of the mountains, as though he could indeed see such a place as Puerta de Luna, and insisted that such a place did exist. He had been there as a boy, but that had been long before the time of the war between the Estados Unidos and Mexico.

A young cowpoke, hunting for strays, had told him that if a cow strayed into that country it was never found again. It was the last thing he had said, over a drink of Ross' good rye, that had interested Ross. He had wiped his mouth and had looked up toward a jagged notch, just north of the pass by which Ross had entered the Rio Dulces Valley less than a week ago. "If there is such a place," he had said thoughtfully, "it is somewhere up near that notch. Funny thing, my brother said he heard a bell there one day just about dusk. I was with him that time. A week later he heard it again. Coupla days later, I was with him in that pass. We was huntin' a mountain

160

lion with the dogs. Jerry claimed he heard that bell again. Nothing for it but what he had to go up there the very next day and find out where it was coming from." The cowpoke had stopped and looked at Ross. "We never saw him again."

Ross rolled a cigarette and lighted it. It was likely that somewhere up there was a place where a man could hide, and where he could have easy access to hidden trails to west and east. A place where there was good shelter, grazing, water and game. A place where one man could stand off a hundred. A man like the Tascosa Kid . . .

The afternoon slowly died. When the dark came Ross slept. The first rays of the full moon tipped the escarpment and shone on his face. He ate his dry food and sat there, while the slow progress of the moon changed lights and shadows on the rugged walls of rock.

He roped and then saddled the dun. He gathered his simple gear and mounted the horse, riding out of the timber into the full light of the moon. In an hour he was in amongst the slope timber and an hour later he had cleared the timberline. Now and then he looked back over his shoulder to gauge the downward progress of the moon, and as he did so he could see far across the great country to the west, over the lower mountains just east of the Jornado del Muerto. Beyond the Jornado was the Rio Grande. The night was almost as bright as daylight.

He found the road an hour before midnight, followed it for half a mile, lost it, then found it again, but this time it ended at a sheer drop, as though thousands of tons of rock, loosened by frost and trickling water, had plunged, long ago, hundreds of feet below, taking the rest of the road with it. Still, it indicated that someone had traveled along the face of the escarpment. Perhaps there *was* something in the legend of Puerta de Luna.

It was close on to midnight when he stopped and slid from the saddle, fashioning a smoke as he scanned the heights above him. Foot by foot he scanned the rough face of the escarpment. He looked back at the dying moon, then back again at the escarpment, and his gaze became fixed on one spot, where the rock seemed different. He looked below it, and there, against the moonlit rock, he saw the faint thread of the road. It had switchbacked somewhere north of where he stood, to gain altitude, and the rock fall had wiped out much of it that had been at Ross' level.

He led the dun up the steep slope, slipping and sliding on the loose rock, making enough noise to awaken the dead. The thought sent a shiver through him. He didn't believe in ghosts and in haunts, but all this talk about a lost village, ghost bells, and vanishing people was enough to set a man's teeth on edge.

The moon was almost gone when he reached the place he had spotted. Begod! There was an opening, at least partway into the living rock. He led the dun into it and in minutes he had lost the light of the moon, although high overhead it still lighted some of the peaks.

By the time the moon was gone, he was floundering through clinging brush and slipping on broken rock, his progress echoing from the high walls on either hand. But now and then he would stumble in ruts on ground that had not yet been covered by rock falls or sliding earth.

The night was pitch dark when at last he felt a strong cold draft on his sweating face. He stopped and peered into the thick darkness ahead of him. He had no idea of what was ahead of him and yet he did not dare light up the lantern he carried on his saddle.

Ross felt for his canteen and tipped it back to drink, and as he did so a cold hand of wind passed over his heated face and the soft, almost indistinguishable ring of a bell came to him. He slowly lowered the canteen and listened, but the sound did not come again. *"If it is heard the third time, the one who hears it is doomed. He will never come out of those mountains,"* Fedro had warned.

"Bull crap," said Ross.

"Bull crap . . . bull crap . . . bull crap . . ." echoed the pass.

He felt for a rock and sat down, nipping now and then at his bottle, chewing on a chunk of cut plug. For some reason or another he did not want to show a light in Puerta de Luna.

The dawn wind crept slowly through the pass. Ross awoke with a start. The false dawn was tinging the patch of eastern sky he could see from where he had spent the night. He stood up stiffly and rubbed his bad knee. Some of his old wounds ached and his bones felt brittle and unyielding. "Jesus, I'm getting old," he grumbled.

"Jesus I'm getting old . . . Jesus I'm getting old . . . Jesus I'm getting old," echoed the pass.

Ross grinned. "Shut up, you bastard," he said.

"Shut up you bastard . . . shut up you bastard . . . shut up you bastard . . ." repeated the pass.

"Right back at me," said Ross in a low voice. "Serves me right."

Breakfast was a slug of rye and a fresh cut of Winesap. By that time the pass was sufficiently lighted by the coming of the dawn for him to be able to pick his way further east, by way of due north, then due south, and once he was downright sure he was heading due west.

The eastern mouth of the pass appeared when he least expected it, as he rounded a sharp bend in the widening pass. He dropped the reins of the dun and took his rifle from the scabbard. The morning sun struck against his face as he walked toward the pass mouth. He stopped and took off his spurs, stuffing them in his pocket. He slanted his hat lower over his face. He crouched behind a rock ledge and studied the lower ground beyond the pass. The road wound across the level ground and disappeared behind a castellated rock formation. There was no sign of life.

Ross led the tired dun across the level ground and left him beside the castellated rocks as Ross scouted on ahead. The ground sloped steadily down toward the east and he walked out upon a wide shelf. Far to his right he could see the dark line that indicated the pass he had taken the day he had first heard the ringing of the bell.

Timber dotted the slopes. The wind shifted, murmuring through the trees, bringing a sharp, winey odor with it. A line of broken rock cut off further view to the east.

He again led the dun forward until he rounded a shoulder of broken rock. He stopped short. A stone building showed on a level area. Part of the roof had collapsed and the door hung on one hinge. Ross walked toward it, looking about for signs of life, but there were none to be seen except for an eagle drifting high against the blue with motionless wings, hunting for his breakfast.

Ross pushed the sagging door to one side and walked inside the building. He started as he saw a grinning skull looking at him with sightless sockets. He walked to the broken bed upon which a dusty blanket covered the bony remains. He drew it back. The man had died fully clothed. A ray of sunlight showing through a window picked out the initials on the big left buckle. J.S. The boots had been removed and the left trouser leg had been slit by a knife. The bones of the upper leg had been cruelly snapped. Ross felt for the makings and rolled a cigarette. Likely the poor bastard had busted his leg up there and had had just enough strength left to get into the old building, but no further. Maybe gangrene had set in. Maybe he had died of hunger and thirst. J.S. The cowpoke who had been hunting for strays had said his brother Jerry had gone up toward Puerta de Luna.

Ross covered the grinning skull and walked outside. He led the dun through the timber and turned to look back, and as he did so, the clear, unmistakable sound of a bell came to him. He dropped the reins and walked quickly forward to the edge of the timber. He narrowed his eyes. "Well, I'll be double-damned!" he said. He took the cigarette from his mouth.

A village stood on level ground, cupped by low hills and knolls. The sun sparkled on a stream that ran past the decaying buildings. Many roofs had fallen in and those that hadn't had sprouted thick green and brown mats of grasses and weeds. At the far end of the street stood a little church, and high in the bell tower he saw a bell. The wind shifted and as it did, the bell rang faintly. "So much for legend," said Ross with a grin.

He left the dun picketed in the thick woods and encircled the deserted village. There wasn't a sign of life about it. The graveyard was unkempt, covered with weeds and drying grass. The footbridge across the stream had long ago collapsed, and the remains had become waterlogged, lying beneath the clear waters.

He walked to the church and entered it through a broken rear door. The place had long ago been stripped of holy pictures and furnishings. He climbed the crumbling bell tower stairs and looked at the ancient bell, greening with age and neglect. The bell rope hung below it. He pushed the heavy rope and the clapper touched the bell, ringing sweetly. The wind had taken over the job of the bell ringer.

Ross shoved back his hat and peered from the bell tower

openings. He could see far beyond the eastern edge of the mountains. That must be Las Piedras where the drift of smoke hung against the clear sky. Far, far to the right and very low he saw the sun sparkling on the Rio Dulces.

Ross went down the stairs and walked out the front door of the church. The street was deserted, but it seemed as though the secretive windows were hollow eyes watching this trespasser.

The sun was slanting westward when he started back for the dun. The horse was gone. Strayed, thought Ross. Damn! It would be a helluva long walk down to civilization, either east or west.

He felt for the makings, and as he did so he clearly saw a bootprint in the softer ground. He studied it. It was too small for his print. He knelt and examined it. The grass was slowly springing back into position. . . . He looked up and studied the quiet woods. Whoever had made that print had been here just a short time ago.

Ross walked toward the edge of the woods. A stone lay with the darker, heavier side upward. He touched it. The dark surface was still damp to the touch and the stone lay in a pool of warm sunlight.

He reached the edge of the woods and looked toward the dreaming village. There was no one there. He walked toward it, wading the shallow stream, and as he reached the far side he saw a pile of droppings at the edge of the street. Steam was still rising from them. Ross picked up a stick and stirred the fresh droppings. There was no trace of oats, but there was grass seed in them. Begod, it wasn't likely his horse that had dropped the pile!

Ross faded back between two buildings. He rubbed his bristly jaws. He reached for the makings and dropped them and as he bent to pick them up a rifle crashed somewhere along the street and a slug smashed against the stone wall just about where Ross' head *had* been. It screamed eerily off into space. Ross dropped flat and rolled over against a wall, shoving his rifle forward. A faint wisp of gunsmoke drifted along the sunlit street. Begod, there *was* someone in this ghost town!

He studied the silent street. Fifty yards down the street he saw the sun glint on something bright. It took him a moment to realize it was the expended hull of the shot that had been fired at him, then ejected to clear the chamber for the next cartridge. Ross wet his dry lips. He inched backward like a crayfish and crawled behind the next building. A bullet skinned the ground a yard from where he lay.

"Kid?" yelled Ross. He immediately rolled over against the building, expecting another bullet.

The village was very quiet after the echoing shots. Ross inched forward and peered around the building. The rifle flatted off from *behind* him. He scuttled around the corner like an ungainly crab and bellied to the front of the building. As he did so he heard someone laughing. "There's a hole in the seat of your jeans, Starkey!" yelled the Kid. "You want me to patch it with a .44/40?"

Cold sweat broke from Ross. Damn him! Where was he! He couldn't possibly move that fast and still keep Ross in sight. Something else struck him; the Kid could have killed him with any of those shots. Ross took the last dregs of his courage in hand and stood up, leaning the rifle against the wall.

"That's a good boy," said the Kid.

"I've got to talk with you," said Ross.

"Why?"

"We went over that the night at the ranch."

"The deal from the governor? Does he really mean it?"

"I've got the papers right here in my pocket."

Minutes ticked past. Ross scanned the roofs of the decaying buildings with narrowed eyes, but there was no sight nor sound of the Kid. If he wasn't a ghost he was the next thing to it.

"You can lower your hands," said the Kid from behind Ross.

Ross turned quickly. The Kid stood there, a rifle at hip level, his cold eyes studying Ross. "I could have killed you half a dozen times since you came pokin' in here."

"Why didn't you?"

"I was curious."

"Where is Miss Maureen?"

"Cross the street. Pass between those two buildings. Keep walking. I'll bring your rifle. I'll be right behind you. Don't make a break, Starkey."

Ross crossed the street and passed between the two buildings. He kept walking toward a motte of timber. He passed into it and then beyond it, then crossed a swale and a low ridge. A large low building of the mission type, but much smaller than those he had seen in other parts of the Southwest and in Mexico, stood beside the stream. Three horses and a pack mule stood in a rude corral. One of them was Ross' dun.

She came to the door as he crossed toward the building. She had changed. She was thinner, seemingly older than when he had last seen her, but as lovely as she had ever been. There was fright in her eyes, as well as relief. Fright for his predicament; relief that the Kid had not killed him . . . yet.

"Are you all right?" he asked.

"Yes," she said quietly. "He hasn't bothered me. He thinks I'm safer up here than at the ranch."

Ross turned and looked at the Kid. There was something different about him too. The Kid jerked his head. "Get into the mission," he said. He grinned. "There aren't any ghosts in there."

The dusty rooms echoed as Ross walked through them with the quiet young woman at his side. They had made their camp in one of the bigger rooms. Saddlebags and a pair of mule aparejos lay against a wall. Cooking gear lay on the wide hearth of a beehive fireplace. A bed had been made in one corner. Maureen looked at Ross. "He has let me have my own room," she said.

"That was nice of him," said Ross.

"Make a meal," said the Kid to the young woman. He took Ross' pistol from its holster and tossed it on top of the bed in the corner. "Set," he said to Ross.

Ross sat down and felt for the makings. He'd never be able to make a break and the Kid knew it. Ross lighted up. He watched the Kid start a fire in the beehive fireplace. "How long do you think you can keep this up, Kid?" he said.

The Kid turned. "They can't get at us up here," he said. "I know every inch of this plateau. I know every hidden trail. Trails that haven't been used for fifty years. I've got guns and ammunition cached in half a dozen places, and extra horses wherever I might need them. Most of the Mexes are my friends. They warn me if anyone is searching for me. I knew you'd eventually find me up here. I could have killed you yesterday or last night, or half a dozen times this morning."

"Why didn't you?"

"Like I said: I was curious. Let me see those papers."

Ross handed the Kid the thick manila envelope. He watched the Kid study the contents. At last the Kid looked up. "Not too bad at that. What do you want me to do?"

"Go back to Santa Fe with me."

The Kid nodded. "That's all, eh?"

"That's it."

"We'll eat first. There will be a fine moon tonight. We can find our way out of here."

Ross studied the Kid. This was too damned easy. The Kid had a poker face. He fashioned a smoke and lighted it. "There's a bottle over there," he said.

"I ain't thirsty."

"That's a switch. You reformin'?"

Ross shrugged. "Maybe."

"I'll bet," said the Kid dryly.

They ate silently. Now and then she would look at Ross with a hidden warning in her eyes, but the Kid at times seemed like his old self. They were drinking their coffee when the sun went down and a cold wind blew across the plateau and moaned through the empty rooms.

The Kid emptied his cup and walked to a window. "Moon will be up before too long," he said.

"We'd better get ready then," said Ross. "We'll need all the time we can get."

The Kid turned. "Why?" he said. "We ain't goin' anywhere."

"What do you mean?" said Ross.

The Kid walked toward the fireplace. He turned. "You damned, conniving liar," he said coldly. "You and your big talk and your phoney papers from the *governor*. Damn you! You think I don't know why you came here?"

Ross stood up. "It's the God's honest truth, Kid!" he said.

"So?" The candlelight shone on the Kid's icy eyes. "What deal did you make with Hardy Newcomb?"

"None! I swear to that!"

"Then how come you're ridin' a horse with a Box HN brand on him?"

Oh, Jesus, thought Ross. I never thought of that.

"You see?" said the Kid slowly. "You can't talk your way out of that one. You'd get me and Miss Maureen out of here and lead us right into a trap like you did her brother."

"You're a damned liar!"

"Yeh?" The Kid laughed softly. "Strange, ain't it, with all them bullets flying, and three of Newcomb's toughest boots there at the mill, plus a few other good guns, *you* happen to be the only one to walk out'a there, untouched."

"He had nothing to do with it, Tascosa," said Maureen.

He looked at her. "Forgive me, Miss Maureen, but you don't know this man. He betrayed your brother and he's betraying me like Judas betrayed Christ."

Ross felt a cold finger of fear trace the length of his spine. The Kid had gone over the edge all right. This was no longer a rational man. Hardy Newcomb, an excellent judge of stock and of men, had hit it right on the nose. "He's gone loco in my opinion," the crippled rancher had said.

The Kid lighted a cigarette and fanned out the match. "I ain't forgot you once saved my life," he said quietly. "I ain't one to kill in cold blood, but I can judge you and condemn you. I'm going to give you your Colt and let you go, with half an hour's start. Then I'm coming to look for you. You can run or you can make a stand, but you might as well know you can't get away."

"Be reasonable, Kid," said Ross.

The Kid took three steps forward and slashed Ross across the mouth with the back of his left hand, drawing blood from Ross' lips. "Git!" he said.

Ross wiped the blood from his mouth. He walked to the bed and got his Colt, knowing better than to turn on the Kid. He walked to the door and turned. "If anything happens to her," he said quietly, "I'll kill you, begod, if I have to come back from the grave!" He left the building, his boots grating on the hard ground in front of the mission, and in a little while the sound died away.

Maureen placed a hand on the Kid's forearm. "Let him go," she said.

The Kid raised his head. "He has to die," he said. "He's in my way. He betrayed me."

"You're betraying yourself," she said. "Tascosa, I love him. Don't you understand?"

He smiled at her. "You just don't understand, do you?"

She shook her head. "No, and I never will." She walked into her dark room and closed the door behind her.

The Kid blew out the candles and sat in the dark, his cold, set face illuminated now and then by the flare of his cigarette tip.

CHAPTER EIGHTEEN

HE STARTED TO RUN and then thought better of it. The fact
that the Kid had said he'd give him a half-hour start didn't
mean a thing. He might be cat footing through the darkness not fifty feet behind Ross.

He walked quickly through the motte, looking back now
and then, trying to distinguish the silhouette of the Kid,
but he saw nothing other than the dim façade of the old
mission and the dark boles of the trees.

He crossed to the first buildings and looked up and down
the street. To hole up would be worse than to run free, and
yet if he kept moving the Kid would see or hear him. He'd
have no chance with the Kid in a draw-and-shoot affair.
With a rifle he might even the odds, but the Kid had the
rifles. Supposing the Kid used a rifle instead of a Colt?
He could shoot just as well with the long gun as he could
with the short.

The thought came to him to make for the pass, but the
moon would be up before he could reach the mouth of it,
and the Kid might already be heading that way to wait
for Ross. Or he might hole up in it and let Ross walk into
the trap.

He could head east toward the lower ground that led
eventually to the Rio Dulces, but he didn't know the lay
of that land at all, and the Kid would know it like the
palms of his hands.

He crossed the street and looked at the church. It had a
front door and a back door, so he wouldn't be trapped in
there, but he'd have to leave either door in the full light
of the moon. He looked up at the bell tower. He could
see the whole village and the approach to it from the

timber from up there, but if the Kid had already started after him, he'd likely see or hear Ross enter the church.

Cold sweat broke from Ross. He looked back over his shoulder. There was no sign nor sound of the Kid, but the man could walk like a hunting cat and shoot in the dark better than most men could shoot in broad daylight.

He stopped between two buildings and tried to think, but the thoughts were a jumbled mess, and panic hovered in amidst them, waiting to take over. "That's just what he wants," said Ross. He looked quickly about. It was almost as though someone else had said it.

He circled around behind the church. The sound of the stream drowned out all other sounds. He bent low and entered the cold water, wading across to the far side. He took cover in the brush while he emptied his boots. He crawled deeper into the brush and beyond it, belly flat his breathing sounding loud enough to be heard fifty yards away, or so he thought.

He saw the western side of the mission beyond a screen of thin timber. More than half an hour had gone past. He could not see the Kid. Foot by foot he worked his way back toward the mission. The wind rose a little, stirring the trees and swaying the dark brush. The faint smell of bittersweet woodsmoke hung in the air. The odor of the horses and the mule came to him.

Ross lay flat, studying the mission. He could get a rifle in there, or at least get a horse, but then again the Kid might have them covered. Damn him! He thought like an Indian.

There was a faint touch of light in the eastern sky. Ross remembered all too well how bright the moonlight was on the plateau. It would be like daylight in less than an hour.

He bellied closer and closer to the mission and at last stood up flat against the eroded wall between two rough buttresses. Gradually he noted that the buttresses were stepped, as though built of successive layers of crude adobe or stones, roughly covered with plaster. He looked up at the edge of the roof, seeing the thick mat of grasses and other growths that thatched it.

Ross wiped the sweat from his face and took off his boots. He tied them together with his scarf and hung them about his neck. Slowly, foot by foot, he worked himself up digging his fingers into crevices, feeling the blood run from his nails, until at last the thatching brushed his sweating face. He pulled himself over the edge and lay flat, breathing hard, feeling the sweat run from every pore. He sat up and pulled on his boots. The light was stronger in the east. The rooftop was thickly layered with the dried grass and weeds. He wondered how strong the roof was. All he had to do was break through and the end would come in a hurry.

He walked softly across the roof until he reached the low wall at the front, part of the curving façade edge, that looked toward the dark motte. There was no movement out there except that of the swaying trees.

He lay flat, taking off his hat, thrusting his head between two clumps of the thick growth. Now there was nothing to do but wait with spidery patience for the Kid to appear, and God help Ross if the Kid knew or suspected that Ross had doubled back on him.

Slowly the full moon arose, lighting first the mountains far beyond the Pecos, then creeping across the Valley of the Pecos to touch the eastern hills of the mountains where flowed the Rio Dulces. Then it flowed across the lower flanks of the mountains and finally covered the mountains themselves, and suddenly Ross could see as clearly as though it was daylight.

He rested his head now and then. He felt unutterably tired. His old wounds ached dully and no matter how he lay they still ached. His bad knee throbbed. I'm getting too old for this game, he thought.

Once she came out of the mission and stood there in the moonlight, not fifteen feet below Ross. She looked toward the village, listening and waiting, and he knew then that the Kid was out there somewhere hunting for Ross. He grinned wryly. Hunt, you smart bastard, he thought.

Once the church bell rang softly. Maybe the Kid was up there.

The moon was slanting down toward the west when one of the horses whinnied softly.

Ross slowly raised his head. A man stood at the edge of the timber, looking to right and to left, and then he crossed the open space toward the mission. Ross tightened his sweaty grip on the Colt butt and his finger took the slack out of the trigger. The Kid was too far away for a clear accurate shot, and Ross wanted him alive.

The Kid stopped and looked back, fifty feet from the front of the mission. He stood there a long time listening.

Ross wet his dry lips. He edged closer to the edge of the roof.

The Kid turned. There was a puzzled look on his handsome face. He walked ten feet.

Ross sat up. The Kid did not look up. He stopped and turned.

Ross rolled over the edge, hung for a second with one hand and then let himself drop. "Grab some sky, Kid!" he cried. He struck heavily and his bad knee gave way. He went down on it as the Kid whirled, clawing for a draw.

For an infinitesimal fraction of time they faced each other, thoughts racing through their minds, and then both of them fired. The Kid grunted in savage pain. He staggered back. Ross leaped to his feet and jumped to one side, fanning the hammer as fast as he could while two slugs whispered past his left ear. Ross' Colt ran dry and the echoes fled across the plateau and died against the moonlit hills.

The Kid stared at Ross with white set face. The smoking Colt dropped from his nerveless fingers. "It had to be *you*," he said hoarsely. "Somehow it ain't right."

Ross lowered his empty pistol. No man alive could stand there with six softnosed .44/40s in his guts.

The Tascosa Kid went down on his knees, and bowed his head as though praying, then he fell face forward and lay still. A slow trickle of blood, black in the bright moonlight, stained the white caliche beneath him.

She came to the mission door. "Are you all right, Ross?" she said.

He nodded dumbly. Slowly he walked to the Kid and rolled him over. Somehow the Kid had died with that fleeting smile on his face, half amused, half sarcastic.

Ross stood up. "Get your things together, Maureen," he said in a toneless voice. He followed her into the echoing mission to help her. "I had to kill him," he said. It was almost as though he was talking to himself instead of to her.

"I know," she said softly.

She came to him, and this time it was her who comforted him. "I'll help you with the ranch," he said.

She shook her head. "I can't ever live there again. I'll sell the Shamrock. We can use the money to buy out your brother."

"You won't find the Canadian like the Rio Dulces," he said.

She rested her head against his chest. "Thank God for that," she said.

Ross loaded the body of the Kid on the mule and carried it to the old graveyard. The moon went down as he began to dig a fresh grave, but he worked by lantern light until the job was done. He rolled the Kid in blankets and tied them about his ankles, knees, waist and neck. He slid the stiffening body into the grave and placed the Kid's engraved and empty Colt atop the body. For a moment he stood there, head bowed in prayer, and then he filled the grave.

They sat silently until the dawn and then rode toward the Door of the Moon. At the edge of the village Ross turned in the saddle. "It's better this way," he said. "I've made a legend of him now. It is what he would have wanted."

Just as they reached the pass, the dawn wind crept across the plateau. Faintly, ever so faintly, came the ringing of the bell.

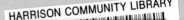